THE WAY OF THE CONDOR

Other books by Nathan Kravetz

Two for a Walk
A Horse of Another Color
(also in French, Hungarian, and Czech editions)
A Monkey's Tale
The Dog on the Ice
He Lost It! Let's Find It!
Is There A Lion In The House?
The Way Of The Condor (also in French edition)

THE WAY OF THE CONDOR

An Adventure in Peru

Nathan Kravetz

AN AUTHORS GUILD BACKINPRINT.COM EDITION

The Way of the Condor
An Adventure in Peru
All Rights Reserved © 1970, 2001 by Nathan Kravetz

No part of this book may be reproduced or transmitted in any form or by any means, graphic, electronic, or mechanical, including photocopying, recording, taping, or by any information storage or retrieval system, without the permission in writing from the publisher.

AN AUTHORS GUILD BACKINPRINT.COM EDITION
Published by iUniverse, Inc.

For information address:
iUniverse, Inc.
5220 S. 16th St., Suite 200
Lincoln, NE 68512
www.iuniverse.com

Originally published by Crown Pulishers
Illustrated by W. T. Mars

ISBN: 0-595-00812-7

Printed in the United States of America

For Deb and Dan

THE WAY OF THE CONDOR

A Glossary at the back of the book gives the meaning of the Spanish words used in this story.

1

CARLOS BERNAL SAT WITH HIS CLASSMATES WAITING FOR the start of the *promoción,* their graduation. On all sides of the schoolyard were his friends and his parents and the other parents and guests.

Far above them all, he saw the grim, jagged peaks of the Andes, patched with green and brown. He saw a circling condor, blending in the sky and then standing out clearly against a white cloud. How much he hoped that he might go where the condor soared, where the world was!

Carlos thought how his school and his teacher had taken him into those mountains and over them. He had learned of the Peruvian land and its rivers and of the mighty ocean that washed its shores. Many of the things Señor Valdez had taught them were things they could not see. And there were still many questions they had not answered.

Carlos' teacher waited for the people to be in their seats so he could begin the graduation. For this day, in honor of the children, friends had come from Cuzco, from Ollantay, even from distant Anta, to the little village of Urubamba.

The men in their *chullos* and dark felt hats were in their seats. The mothers and girls with their many petticoats and broad velvet hats with colored tassels sat beside them.

The murmuring of the many voices gradually grew still. The *promoción* class of ten boys and three girls was in its place. A hushed silence gave an atmosphere of dignity and

seriousness to the schoolyard. In the morning light, the whitewashed adobe school looked clean and fresh. Its wooden door was open and the two windows without glass let light into the bare room. The wooden tables and benches were in order, and the year was indeed finished. All that remained was the ceremony for the *promoción.*

In front of the building, on chairs facing their families and neighbors, sat the *alumnos,* soon to be *ex-alumnos,* with their teacher. The boys in their khaki uniforms, the girls in dark blue, looked alert and serious.

Carlos glanced at his friend Ricardo as they sat beside each other with their hands on their knees. Carlos remem-

bered how they had both started in the Urubamba school four years ago. Barefoot, in khaki cap and uniform, Carlos had seen Ricardo standing beside him. Carefully they had eyed each other then, while the parents spoke softly together about their flocks of sheep and their small crops of maize.

And now it was already their last day in the school, the *promoción*. Parents, sisters and brothers, even the *abuelitos,* the grandfathers and grandmothers, were there.

Carlos thought sadly that if only his older brother, Edmundo, could be here, too, the day would be perfect. But he would write to Lima and tell Edmundo all about it.

Now it was time to begin.

Señor Valdez stood up. He walked briskly to the flagpole where he and the mayor, Alcalde Don Diego, attached the national flag of Peru to the lines.

They pulled the lines and the wind caught the rising red and white banner, giving it fullness. The people stood up when the flag reached the top and then streamed out in the brisk Andean breeze.

The Urubamba town band sounded the opening chords of the national anthem, and the voices of the pupils led in the singing:

"*Somos libres, seamos lo siempre . . . !* We are free, let us be so forever . . . !"

For many of the adults of the Indian village, the Spanish words were not easy, and they tried in their own way to sing this important song. Yet it was the children, young and strong, who kept the music going and brought it to its climax.

When all was quiet again, Señor Valdez stepped to the front of his *promoción* class to begin the program.

"Welcome, dear friends," he began.

He said the customary words of greeting to the Alcalde, to the worthy ladies and gentlemen who had come from great Cuzco, to the parents of the pupils, to their friends and families, and finally, to the pupils themselves.

Señor Valdez stood straight as he spoke. His dark hair was over his eyes sometimes, but his glance was sharp and clear.

As Carlos listened, he remembered how this man had come among them nearly five years ago. They had had an old teacher whose health was bad, and when Señor Valdez came to them from Lima, they were uneasy.

He wore his suit with a shirt and a tie. His skin was dark as theirs was, but he spoke the language of the city and they were not sure of him.

The school building was dirty; the adobe had cracked and fallen. He fixed and cleaned, brought new benches and desks, and when school opened, he waited for his pupils.

Only a few boys came and he greeted them. Señor Valdez was young and strong and he worked as long as the sun gave light, for there was no other in the school. He drew pictures and wrote numbers on any paper that he could find. He repainted the blackboard and wrote words on it for his pupils. He spoke softly and with kindness.

Gradually they worked together, learned, and became a school.

To all he spoke in Spanish, but when he visited the little farms where the children lived, or the shops in the town, he spoke to the fathers and the grandfathers in Quechua, the ancient tongue. To the youngest children he also spoke in Quechua, the language their mothers used and the Incas before them.

More and more, the children came to the school of Señor Valdez, mostly boys, but even a few girls. When a father had time, or in passing the school on his way to the town, he would stop and hear the classes at their reading. He could hear the children learning from the books and the map that Señor Valdez had received from the Ministry of Education in far-off Lima.

As a stranger he had come to them, but he was strong in his knowledge and wise in his ways. He spoke to them in Spanish and in their ancient Quechua, and for those fathers who wanted to learn this same reading that the children knew, Señor Valdez was at the school early, with the rising sun.

On the day of the *promoción* that first year, a "treasure" was brought to the school—a kerosine lamp. Señor Valdez, whose candles were bright enough for his own reading and writing, now could have a small class in the evening also. This gift from the parents, who could hardly spare their children for the school, brought them their time for learning, too.

Now, for Señor Valdez who had been a stranger, there were no strange names or faces. He was a teacher of children and a teacher of families. His teaching had reached out beyond the reading and the writing and the history of Peru. From Señor Valdez had come ways to keep clean, ideas for good diet, and, with these, respect and a sense of responsibility for the school.

Carlos and his friends, during the four years that he was in the little school, had learned many things. They read, they wrote, they studied maps, learned the Catholic teachings, and they sang their country's anthem. And they often talked about the times and deeds of Simón Bolívar and San Martín, the national heroes.

Carlos thought of this as he heard the teacher speak.

"Dear friends and honored guests," said Señor Valdez. "On this special day many have come from far away to see us. Although they do not visit with us often, we are happy when they do."

Señor Valdez looked with a warm smile toward the front row of seats where the mayor sat with the visitors from Cuzco.

He then invited Padre Manya, the priest of the town and his good friend, to bless the meeting.

The young priest stood before the crowd and spoke the familiar words, "In the name of the Father, and of the Son, and of the Holy Spirit . . ." He prayed for the town and for the nation.

But, when he might have sought the blessing for "our teacher, Victor Valdez," he asked instead for the "blessing of learning" for the children. A new prayer, thought some. An unusual request!

Then, after the prayer, he blessed them again and

strode firmly to his seat, his robes rustling as he moved.

Señor Valdez spoke again, this time inviting the representative of the *prefecto,* or governor, at Cuzco to address them.

Up rose a thin man, small, with a small moustache and a high piercing voice. He spoke rapidly and told them of his many tasks. He reminded them of the difficulties the prefect of a department may have.

He also referred often to the great feats of the Inca Empire and to the vast domains of the nation, gazing all the while at the paper in his hands.

In this audience no heads nodded and no eyes closed. In fact, among the members of the graduating group, there were a few open mouths. Carlos nudged Ricardo and whispered, "You hear? All those things to see! So much to do!" And so it seemed indeed.

Following the talk of the prefect's aide, Señor Valdez called upon the next person in order, the Alcalde, mayor of Urubamba. This gentleman, being somewhat old and tired, was not anxious to make a long speech. Instead, he spoke briefly and used almost the same words as the visitor from Cuzco. He added, however, a few extra thoughts with which all seemed to agree:

"I find great satisfaction in the visit of our friends from the great city. I hope they will come again soon. May their journey be pleasant and the road smooth. In fact, we are looking forward to improvements in the road to Cuzco which will make it so. They have assured us of this, and I know we shall not need to wait long."

Hearing this, Carlos' father shrugged his shoulders. Many times they had spoken of the need to repair the once-firm highway of the Incas. In many places the rains had washed away the flat stones that had at last been loosened and broken by the heavy trucks and buses. And yet, there had been no work on the famous highway except that done by the villagers, when they could spare the time from their lands and flocks.

So, once again, a gentle reminder was being made in the ear of the *prefecto's* aide. Whether there would be a reply in the form of machinery, materials, and workmen, remained to be seen. Until then, trucks would break axles and springs in dry weather, dumping people and cargoes. In the rainy season they would be stuck in the deep mud or go sliding off the road. At such times there were usually no drivers brave enough or willing to risk their vehicles for the trip.

With most of the speeches ended, Señor Valdez called upon the children to sing again. Several groups of the pupils, including the very youngest, went through the graceful dance, the *marinera*. As the little band played, each dancer waved his colored strip of llama fur. The partners moved about each other, gracefully crossing the *reatas*, twisting them and exchanging them as they danced.

The parents smiled and tapped their feet to the strains of the music. They too danced the *marinera* and other dances more ancient.

Now Carlos saw Señor Valdez reach for the certificates as he began to call the names of his graduating students. Solemnly, the soon-to-be-*ex-alumnos* stood: ten boys in clean khaki shirts, trousers, and caps; three girls in dark blue skirts and white blouses, their hair hanging down in thick braids.

Carlos looked at his father, his *taita*, and then at his mother and at his sister Martita. He knew they were pleased with him and proud.

He took a sharp breath when he heard at last, "Bernal, Carlos!"

"Present!" he called. Then walking to the front table, he looked into his teacher's eyes, gripped his hand, and returned to his place.

Each year Carlos had attended this ceremony, and now it was for him. He had seen his friends and schoolmates who would have nothing more to do in the school. For them, in Urubamba, there was no school after those first four years.

What could be done? Carlos knew now that boys and girls who were to better themselves and their country would have to go on to finish the elementary grades and then go further. They would go on to high school and later to the university, or to the teacher-training colleges or the special institutes for engineering or agriculture.

He thought of the boys and girls, even the very bright ones, who left school and returned to the land and the small flocks. Some drifted away to Cuzco, to Huancayo, to Arequipa, to Lima. But without schooling they went only to find work and to remain ignorant. Often they forgot the little they had learned and lost interest in schooling.

This day, too, as he and his friends waited in their seats he wondered what might be done.

Then he heard his teacher say, "Friends, I want to send our *ex-alumnos* forth with my best wishes and I know yours go with them."

"I have another wish, however. I wish that we were not sending them out of school at all. It is certainly time, I think, to ask for a better road to Cuzco. It is also time to ask for a better road to learning and knowledge."

Expecting the usual remarks of farewell that the teacher made every year, some of the audience were preparing to leave. Now they stopped. They were not sure they had heard correctly.

"What did he say?" whispered the Alcalde to Padre Manya.

"One moment," replied the priest, "he is just beginning."

"Yes," continued Señor Valdez, "when we have only

four years of school for our children, we are giving them too little for their journey in life.

"They can go no further in helping themselves or their families, or our beloved country. Without learning, our children are prevented from finding their talents and their true future. Why should they not have the opportunity of the child in Cuzco or in the capital? They should be able to complete at least the full six years of elementary school and then go even further.

"This is my thought: that when you think of a better road for trucks, will you not also think of a school of *segundo grado,* of six years, for the children of our town and of what it could mean?"

As his teacher spoke, Carlos looked around and saw on many faces a questioning look. On some faces, however, he saw dark anger and disapproval.

But when he looked at his classmates and at the parents, he saw mostly nods in agreement, smiles, and eyes that sent gratitude.

Then Carlos heard Señor Valdez' closing words of appreciation to the guests for their interest in the children. He again offered his good wishes and congratulations to the graduates and their families. Then, motioning to Padre Manya to give his blessing, Señor Valdez stood by as the meeting ended.

As the children moved to join their parents, the murmurs arose on all sides. The voice of Don Manuel, who owned the largest hacienda near Urubamba, could be heard clearly.

"Four years of school are surely enough for a child of Urubamba! What more should he need to work on the land or in the town?"

"Of course," replied Señor Rivera, the storekeeper. "We all know that with too much learning they forget their place. They become too busy with reading and other such tricks."

Don Diego, the alcalde, answered softly, "Well, for girls, perhaps, but our boys are as smart as any in Peru. We ought to do more for them."

"Indeed," said the governor's aide, who was getting ready to leave. "For those of us whose families have always helped to govern, education *is* important. I'm not so sure we really want too many overeducated people. Especially those who are only now beginning to change from speaking Quechua to Spanish. There is plenty of time for more than that."

Carlos noticed that Señor Valdez glanced at Padre Manya who stood at his side. As their eyes met, there was a quick smile. Then they stepped forward to greet the parents of the pupils, and others whose voices they had not yet heard.

2

IN THE NEXT WEEKS WHENEVER PEOPLE OF THE VILLAGE met, they talked about the school. Arguments arose among them and voices sometimes became shouts.

As for the children themselves, some looked upon Señor Valdez' suggestion with doubts.

"After all," said one of the boys, "if I could only stay out of school altogether, my life could be so free!"

"Certainly," answered Carlos, "as free as those sheep you tend. Don't you want to learn more and make something of yourself?"

"Not at all!" shouted another. "I want to go to Lima and become a great man there. Surely anyone could do that in Lima!"

"Ay," sighed Carlos, looking sideways at Ricardo. His friend would, indeed, be on his way to Lima. He only waited for word from his sister who worked in the capital.

How he had talked about it! How he looked forward to finding his sister Sarita, who worked in the great city. There Ricardo was going also—whether to work or to go to school, he did not know.

Sarita had written that there was much a boy could do in Lima, and she had promised to send the fare for Ricardo to come after the *promoción*. "You can work in a great house," she had said. "And maybe someday you will be the *mayordomo*, in charge of everything!"

"Or you can work in a shop, in a store, in a factory. There are so many places!" Sarita had written.

"Many boys work, Ricardo. But maybe . . . maybe you would also go to school. You could learn to be an engineer, or a doctor, and then what a great man our Ricardo would be!"

"Yes," Ricardo had said. "What a wonderful world Lima must be!"

The boys had talked much of this time after the *promoción*, but for Carlos everything was in doubt. He wished with all his heart to be able to go with his friend. But it could not be.

The discussions and arguments continued in the village. Most of the people did want more education for their children. But some who were close to Don Manuel and to Señor Rivera did not agree that the town needed six years of elementary school.

Meanwhile, during the next weeks, Carlos and Ricardo worked as before, on the land and with their fathers. But whenever they could, they would climb together into the hills above the village. Or they would sit beside the swift-flowing Vilcanota River which passed near the town.

One day, after a rain, they walked along the road, barefooted, enjoying the cool air.

"How I would like to go to Lima with you, Ricardo!"

"What fun we would have! You could stay with Sarita and me. And we could see all of Lima together."

"Well, what's the use of talking about it. I can't go anyway. I have no sister there."

"Maybe Edmundo has a job in Lima now. You could stay with him."

"No, Ricardo, I don't think so. In his last letter, he wrote that he was driving a truck from Lima to Huancayo. Edmundo has seen many places, but he likes to keep moving. Someday, he said, he will even drive a truck to Iquitos!"

"Hah," grinned Ricardo, "not unless he drives it up and down half the rivers of Peru, since there are no roads to Iquitos! Your brother is quite a joker!"

"Well, he is—but if anyone ever does drive a truck to Iquitos, I know it will be Edmundo, in spite of the jungle!"

Carlos wished that he could have written to Edmundo about his hopes, that he wanted so much to see Lima and the people there. But he knew that he would have to stay with his father after the *promoción*.

Even while he was a schoolboy, Carlos had spent many

hours with his father, tending the fields, gathering the stones so they could plow a careful and straight furrow. He helped with the planting, with the harvest, and with the drying of the corn before it would be sent to the Cuzco millers.

Carlos knew that his parents were proud of his ability to read and write, but he also knew that he had done well in his work, farming, tending the sheep and the three llamas.

The time passed only too slowly for Ricardo. The end of school was already three weeks past, and he had become very gloomy. His talks with Carlos were more and more listless. Even his jokes and good humor were nearly gone.

In this mood, the two boys came back one late afternoon from tending their flocks together. As Carlos moved his sheep farther down the road toward his father's corral, Ricardo went halfheartedly into his own. Then, with a brief wave, he went into the house.

Carlos was just a short distance down the road when he heard a loud yell. He turned around. There he saw Ricardo shouting, dancing down the road after him, waving a sheet of paper.

"It's here, Carlito! It's here! My letter from Sarita has come at last!"

Carlos turned and waited for him. Then, as Ricardo came up to him, he said, forcing a smile to his face, "You see, I told you it would come."

"Yes," replied Ricardo gleefully. "And now, all I have to do is write that I will come. Then, off I go! Whoosh!"

By this time, Ricardo's mother and father and his little brothers had come out of the house. They stood on the road, waiting for him to get over some of his excitement, and then they waved at Carlos and went back inside.

"Well, Ricardo, I'd better get back home. I know you have plenty to do now."

"Of course," answered Ricardo somewhat thoughtfully, "I'll get started on that letter to my sister first."

That night as the family had their evening meal, Carlos told of Ricardo's letter from Lima and his plan to leave within a few days.

"Ay," sighed his mother. "There are treasures and wonders everywhere. So there must be some in Lima, too."

"Mama," interrupted Martita, "I would be afraid to go so far from home. And they say it is so hot near the great ocean."

Carlos said little more. He ate in silence and cast occasional glances toward his father, who also continued his meal without speaking.

The next morning Carlos and his father walked to their fields. They looked so much alike, with their strong, curved noses and straight black hair. They showed their Inca ancestry in their slender bodies and bronzed skin.

Carlos thought of this once again as he walked beside his father, looking at the poncho, the knee-length black trousers, and the leather sandals which moved surely and lightly over the ground as they went.

They started out in silence, but as they climbed steadily, his father looked at him from time to time, studying his son's face.

As a person who rarely showed his emotions, Carlos' father wondered over his son who did.

This boy, he thought, who works with me as a man, has already learned some new ways. Our ways are already different. I see his face light up and his eyes dance, and I know he is happy. When he is silent and his face is still, anyone can read his thoughts.

"*Churi,*" he said, with the ancient Quechua words, "we have a long way to go."

"*Ari, taita,* yes, father. But I don't mind the long climb to the land. We shall be there soon."

"Of course," said his father thoughtfully, "but I am thinking of how far Ricardo goes and how far you may go."

"Yes, my father, Ricardo will soon go to Lima. I would give much to go with him."

"That is something we must speak about. I can read your thoughts on your face. It is easy to know what you feel."

"But father, now that I have finished school I should not stay. What has been the use of learning if I must end so soon and then forget it all?"

"True, but that is because there is no more school here for you. Even so, if you went to school for two more years, you would surely want to leave then."

"That is so, *taita*. I would want to go to high school and continue to learn. But, what's the use? I know I am needed here for my help to you and my mother. Edmundo has gone, and the work is too much for one man."

His father smiled and turned away. Surely the work was too much for one man. But who, in truth, had done it while the children were small? And who could still do it, not very easily, but well enough?

Yet no family wanted to send a young son away to work among strangers. While Ricardo could go to his sister, Carlos had no one. It would be improper to send him along as a burden to Sarita with Ricardo. No, his work was useful. It was a man's work truly. Carlos was needed, and as long as the food was sufficient, the soil rich, and the skies bountiful, they would manage.

Carlos remained Ricardo's close companion and he listened with weak enthusiasm to his friend's plans. They went over and over all the things Ricardo would do, his visits to the sea, to the great plazas of Lima, to the President's Palace, the congress, the cathedral, all the wonderful places about which Señor Valdez had talked and read to them.

In all their plans, Ricardo promised there would be a

place for Carlos. He would work and would find a job for Carlos, too. They would be together, and soon.

At the little town plaza two days later, clusters of people surrounded a small stake truck, with the dignified name of *El Águila Real, The Royal Eagle,* over the cab.

Always, the boys had talked of the trucks that passed through Urubamba with the bold names on their hoods or over the windshields on the cabs. There was the *Poderoso,* the *Mighty One.* There was the great red and blue *Águila Azul,* the *Blue Eagle.* And then just *León I* and *León II,* two noble lions.

The trucks had many names and so did the buses, but they hardly spoke of the buses. These long, shiny "houses of many windows" carried people who could pay more than fifteen *soles* for the trip. To ride a bus meant to have a seat and a roof, with windows that closed and helped you to stay warm. Well, who could think of a bus, when you knew that everyone in your town went to Cuzco on a truck, or to Abancay, or even as far as Huancayo?

But always the talk had made them see in their minds the great capital, Lima, and Carlos would dream of a mighty truck with the name *Libertador, Liberator,* which would carry him to Lima.

Now, the *Eagle* waited for its standing passengers to Cuzco, and this day Ricardo would be among them.

His mother and father stood by solemnly. His mother in her bright shawl and a high white hat looked often at the bundle her son held. She had put dried beef, cold potatoes, some corn, and bread into the sack. In a small bag, too, she had secretly placed a *sol* coin, saved and guarded carefully for just such a time.

His father wore a poncho over an old jacket, and on his head was a dark felt hat. He had said his words of advice and caution to Ricardo already. He himself had never been beyond Cuzco, let alone to Lima, but he had given his counsel to his son. There was no more to say except *"Vaya con Dios."*

The rest of the family, the little children, stood nearby and held onto their mother's wide skirts. Their eyes shone with the wonder of their brother's great adventure. They would miss his jokes and stories, but they saw how happy he was.

Ricardo and Carlos stood near the truck and hardly spoke at all. Ricardo, too, wore a poncho over an old jacket. He wore no hat, although in his cloth sack were a *chullo* with colorful ear flaps and a long tassel as well as a felt hat like his father's. The bundle was quite small, for Ricardo's belongings were few.

At last it was time. The driver impatiently sounded the horn as his assistant began to help the people up into the truck. This boy, no older than Ricardo, was known as the *chulillo* but he preferred to be called the *copiloto* because he sometimes rode beside the driver.

"Quickly, quickly," he urged the people. "The *piloto* is ready to go now. Here is your bag, señora. Come, *chico,* I'll give you a hand."

The boy was everywhere, busily getting people on the truck, handing them their bundles, keeping an eye always on the driver to see if he was becoming impatient.

Ricardo embraced each of his little brothers in turn, then finally his mother and father. They held his hands briefly and looked into his eyes solemnly.

"Go with God," they murmured, and they released him.

Ricardo and Carlos looked at one another. Then, swiftly, they embraced and clenched each other's hands.

"Goodbye, friend," said Carlos. "May all go well with you."

"Goodbye, Carlito," replied Ricardo.

Quickly he turned away and strode to the truck. Disregarding the hand of the *chulillo* held out to help him, he pulled himself up briskly and moved along the side of the truck where he could be near the cab.

With a final blast of the horn, the truck slowly moved away from the people in the little plaza.

Carlos stood alone and waved in farewell, watching the truck as it left clouds of dust in the mountain air.

A few days later, Carlos sat in a mountain meadow tending his flock. He watched as they grazed slowly, seeking the tenderest grasses of the *altiplano*. He sat there and filled the valley with the high, reedy notes of the *quena*, his flute.

As the notes of the *quena* drifted across the land, they caught the ear of a man who was climbing from one of the adobe huts below. He moved as if pulled by the boy and his flute. Surefooted, he climbed over the clumps of stones and the crackling brush of the *altiplano*. From time to time, he stopped to lift his old felt hat, and he wiped his hand across his warm face. The climb, slow as it was, tired him, but as he approached the boy, his steps quickened and his shoulders under the poncho seemed straighter.

As he climbed nearer the flock, his movements caught the boy's eye. The music stopped. Then, as if uncertain, the boy stood up. He shaded his eyes to see better. The man came nearer, and suddenly the boy's shout rang over the valley.

" 'Mundo! 'Mundo!"

He raised his hand, calling loudly, " 'Mundo!"

Then, waving his flute, he scrambled downhill toward the man, shouting as he leaped over brush and stones.

The two came together and stopped. Carlos, in excitement, reached up to embrace his older brother.

" 'Mundo! You're back! You're back!" he repeated.

As the two looked at each other, Edmundo said softly,

"Ay, Carlito, how much you have grown. How strong you are, and how tall!"

The brothers, one still a boy, the other already a man, spoke with warmth and friendliness. That was how it had been with them always. Edmundo, the older, strong and kind, had been a companion to Carlos. He, too, had been in school for four years, then returned to the land and the work it demanded.

But 'Mundo, filled with desires to see more and to know more, had found a way to go out into the world. As a helper on a truck, a *chulillo,* he had left his village to ride the rough, tortuous roads of the Andean passes. Loading cargo, shifting sacks and boxes, learning, always learning, Edmundo was, within a year, a driver, a *piloto*.

His restless eyes continually scanned the roadway. He knew how to use his deft hands for emergency repairs on the trucks and yet he had strength to grip the wheel for turns around sweeping, treacherous curves. He had worked for a company in Lima which carried cargoes of many kinds from all parts of Peru to the capital. As a trusted driver, he commanded his own helpers. He was a respected friend and co-worker. When he drove the truck *Dios y Patria,* no cargo was safer, no schedule better kept.

In the midst of his rejoicing, Carlos had a strange, worried feeling. He knew that all was not well with his brother. But surely, all *was* well. Edmundo's smile was the same—reserved, honest. But Carlos noticed something unclear in his brother's eyes, something tired and troubled.

" 'Mundo," he asked as they walked slowly toward their house, "how long can you stay with us? Are you on a trip to Cuzco with your truck? How fine it is to see you again!"

Edmundo was silent. Then his answer chilled Carlos, as he said, "I have no truck now. I have come home."

That evening after the meal, Edmundo told his family of the great capital and the broad endless ocean. The children and their parents listened eagerly as he described the streets and plazas which resounded with clanging bells of street cars, noisy horns of cars and trucks, and the crowds of bustling people.

In his truck he had driven along the great *Panamericana,* the highway that stretched from one end of Peru to the other, and that ran like a string to the lands in the north and the south.

"I have been in Arequipa, the White City, which is guarded by Misti, a sleeping volcano. And I have driven without fear across the great desert near our border with Ecuador.

"In Lima I have seen bullfights with *toreros* from Spain, and matches of *fútbol* with teams from Mexico. I have brought monkeys and snakes from the jungle of Tingo Maria. Once I sat in my truck for five days, along with seventy other trucks, waiting for the jungle road to be repaired."

Carlos sat spellbound as his brother talked. All those places! All the people and the cities! No wonder he himself hated the day-after-day life on the land.

His father sat listening, too, a bit uncertain of what he had heard. No one, he felt, needed to leave the farming and the flocks. This son of his had become almost a stranger. He had done much, but such work was not really important. It was the land, always the land, which must be tended. The land provided well for the man who worked it with care. If only the rains and the sun . . .

But his sons were not happy with the land and the work it demanded. They saw the wide horizons and gazed longingly beyond the mountains.

Yet, as he wondered, he felt he must ask his son a question.

"Edmundo, how long will you stay now? Where is your truck?"

All grew still, and on Edmundo's face they saw a shadow pass over his excitement. He paused and then, looking into the small fire in the courtyard, he licked his lips. His shoulders slumped and he spoke with hesitation.

"I have no truck. In Lima I became ill. I could not work, and my comrades among the drivers cared for me. They shared some of their wages to help me. But I was too weak and they were too poor to keep me with their families."

His mother cast down her eyes and rocked herself gently, murmuring, *"Pobrecito,"* as if Edmundo were still her little child.

"One day," continued Edmundo, "my friends took me to the government hospital. The doctors and the nurses cared for me until I became stronger. When I left the hospital, the doctor said I must leave Lima until I become well again. I should return to the mountains where the air is clear and dry. The weather in Lima is not healthful, and we people of the *altiplano* are sometimes made weak there when we work strenuously. But I wanted very much to return to my truck and once again follow the highways and the mountain roads.

"When I returned to the company, my job was gone. Another *piloto* had been hired, and I had to look elsewhere. I went all over Lima, to all the companies who used drivers. But there was no real job for me, and none of my former comrades could help me to find one. Besides, I still remembered the words of the doctor.

"So, *taita,* I have come home, and I will work our land with you, if there is food enough."

His father stood up and, without a word, put his hand on his son's shoulder. With this welcome, he left the room.

3

THE DAYS PASSED MORE QUICKLY FOR CARLOS NOW. HE, HIS father, and Edmundo worked their land, tended the flock, helped in the home, and went to the Sunday market in the village. They also worked on the lands of Don Manuel as their obligations and debts required.

One Sunday, after they had loaded a few kilos of potatoes onto the back of the black-and-white llama, the family joined the others in the plaza of Urubamba. There, under the clear blue sky, the women set out their little stocks of vegetables on the ground and waited for customers to buy or exchange.

Marta stayed with her mother while Edmundo, Carlos, and their father walked off to join the men who sat together in another part of the plaza.

They were greeted pleasantly with slight nods, and soon they were occupied in their favorite pastime—a conversation of many silences. One man spoke briefly about the weather. There was a long interval of silence. Then another man agreed. Again, long silence. Then, soon, another comment. This time, perhaps it was on another subject such as crops, or the condition of the soil, or the flow of the river.

Some of the men, from time to time, reached into the decorated pouches they wore at their belts and took a pinch of coca leaves to add to the mouthfuls they were chewing.

As the men leaned with their backs to the wall of the old church, Señor Valdez walked by and greeted them.

"Good morning, señores," he said, and then, noticing Carlos, he smiled and added, "Carlos, how are you?"

Carlos replied, "I am well, sir, thank you."

"You have not come to see me lately," added the teacher. "I would be glad if you would."

"Well, sir," answered Carlos with a shy smile, "I will come soon."

"I've just received some books and a few newspapers from Lima," said Señor Valdez. "I know you want to keep up with your reading."

He nodded politely and was about to leave when he stopped and said to the men, "I've just remembered something. In one of the newspapers there was a report about visitors who would come to Cuzco and the towns nearby, perhaps even to Urubamba."

The men looked at Señor Valdez with new curiosity. Visitors were rare in the town although tourists from Cuzco occasionally passed through on the way to the Macchu Picchu ruins.

"Who are these visitors, Señor Valdez?" asked Edmundo.

"According to the report," he replied, "they are officials of the Ministry of Public Education in Lima. They will be studying the schools and meeting with the teachers."

One of the other men asked the teacher a question:

"Señor Valdez, are you going to have a meeting of these officials and the *padres de familias,* the parents of the schoolchildren? We have not forgotten some of your own words at the *promoción.*"

"Well," said the teacher in a dry voice, "I'm sure they will be too busy, but after visiting the school, they usually meet with the alcalde for refreshments."

With that, he said, *"Con permiso,"* and walked off, a slight smile drifting about his lips.

The noises of the market floated across the plaza. Voices of women over their bargains were soft and melodious. Children's voices were shrill and joyous. And the conversation among the men grew animated, with fewer silences than before.

In a short time, word reached Urubamba. The official visitors would be coming on Wednesday. During the remaining days of the week, everything went very slowly for Carlos. Time dragged. The sheep dragged. Even the great soaring condor seemed to falter in his flights across the valley.

Edmundo scolded him gently once when he seemed to be more excited than ever about the visitors.

"Come on now, boy, the sun will rise and set on time. No need to be so agitated!"

"But think, Edmundo," answered Carlos, "they'll be coming all the way from Lima to see our school. I once went to that school, you know."

"Well, that is so!" replied Edmundo with a smile. "But I came from Lima just to see you—and see how I work now?"

"Besides," he added, "I went to that school also, and now we work alongside our *taita* who never needed school to learn how to pull stones from the soil!"

On Wednesday, the day's work ended early in all the Urubamba valley. In the soft dusk, families strolled toward the school as if it were *promoción* time once more. A few carried small kerosine lanterns, but most walked the road for they had just left their fields.

When they reached the school, they saw an automobile standing in the road beside the wall. On the door of the car was painted an unusual insignia. Carlos did not understand what it meant, but he saw a shield on which two hands clasped each other. The shield was decorated on its lower half with red and white stripes. Above the clasped hands were blue stars. And below the shield were the words CUERPO DE PAZ.

Carlos and his family were standing beside the car when the driver who had been sitting inside leaped out quickly and opened the rear doors. Accompanied by Señor Valdez were two men and a woman, all very ordinary-looking. But the men wore fine white shirts, and neckties besides! And the woman was dressed in a suit such as the tourists often wore.

The people heard them thank the teacher as they entered their car with its unusual insignia on the door. One of the visitors was also unusual, for his *"Muchas gracias"* sounded strange to Carlos who heard him speak to the teacher.

He must be a real *Limeño,* thought Carlos. He doesn't even speak Spanish as we do.

As the car drove off to the village, Carlos and the others followed.

Coming to the plaza before the alcalde's house, the people of the town remained dignified and almost without expression on their faces. They were, after all, only observers on such occasions, not participants.

Carlos saw that Señor Valdez stood to one side with Padre Manya as the visitors talked with the alcalde. A few of the people began to whisper among themselves, and Carlos saw one of them point toward the palest of the strangers, the one whose strange Spanish he had heard at the school.

"Gringo," someone said, and pointed again at the man.

"Gringo," repeated others, but this word meant nothing to Carlos.

Just then the alcalde, Don Diego, came forward. He welcomed the visitors, and then he reached out to shake the hand of the older man.

The man whose hand he had taken spoke simply and directly to the people as well as to their mayor. And his words came to Carlos' ears as a refreshing breeze.

"My colleagues and I," he said, "have come from the Ministry of Public Education. This is Señorita Palomino, a specialist in primary education. I am Luis Lopez. My work is also in primary education. We are teachers, and it is our task to help teachers.

"We are here with a good friend. This is Señor Dr. Taylor, who has come from the United States of America. He is also our colleague and has worked with us both as a teacher and a friend. His country has sent him to learn about our ways and to share his knowledge and his experience with us.

"On our trip from Lima, we have been visiting the

schools of this region. We know that many schools need improvement, and we want to help."

Suddenly someone interrupted, "But sir," it was Señor Rivera, the storekeeper, "nothing needs to be done. Other towns may have problems. Other towns may even lack a school. But in our Urubamba, we have a school and no need for improvement."

A murmur arose among the people. Some heads nodded in agreement, but most of the men said nothing aloud. Carlos wondered what Señor Lopez would think now.

He spoke again, with a look first at the alcalde, and then to the people:

"If you are satisfied and content, we shall note that . . ."

Just then Carlos heard another voice: "No, señor, we cannot be content!"

This was a voice he knew. It was Edmundo, his brother, who spoke now, caring little for the dark glances of Señor Rivera and of a few others.

"How can we say we are satisfied," asked Edmundo, "if our teacher labors in a single room with the children of all the grades? When a boy of Urubamba finishes his fourth year, his education is over. Should we say this is enough? I, too, have been to Lima, and I know. Our people need learning, and without it we cannot be content! We shall prepare a petition for our government in Lima and ask for what is needed in Urubamba!"

Edmundo stopped, but the murmuring rose in force, and it suddenly grew noisy in the plaza.

The alcalde was about to speak again, but just then Carlos saw the stranger from that distant land step forward. He stood silently, and in the crowd some of the voices could be heard saying, *"Gringo."*

Carlos looked at the man and saw him raise a hand. Age-old traditions of courtesy had their effect. The crowd fell silent when Dr. Taylor spoke.

His words came slowly, and they did not always sound correct to the ears of the people. But their meaning was clear.

"Friends," he said, "we have come to your land"—he used the warm word *tierra*—"to study... We want to do more than study—we want to understand and to help. As the young man told us, education is important. It has been so in my country. For your nation and community it is so, too. I am sure if you prepare a petition, your government will give its attention and its help."

The crowd stood respectfully as Dr. Taylor finished and stepped into the shadows beside Padre Manya and the teacher. His simple words had reached them and they had no anger for anyone.

The people began to move about, whispering together, leaving the plaza for their homes. But before they could go, Señor Lopez came forward and spoke once more:

"The words of our friend come from his understanding of Peru and its people. Do you see on this car the sign with the clasped hands? This means that we are joined by our neighbors in the north as friends and brothers. Do you see the words *Cuerpo de Paz?* With these words we mean a Peace Corps of Peruvian and North American teachers who are interested in the needs of our children. In our work we need the facts and the time to study them. Send your petition and then you shall hear more of our plans. I give you my thanks for us all. Good night!"

The people smiled as they went to their car. Carlos stood up on tiptoe. Here were friends of the *campesinos* and their words were reassuring.

The next afternoon, before the sun went down, Carlos was at the school with Edmundo and a number of the other young men who felt that something must be done about the school in Urubamba.

But many of the people were afraid to differ with Don

Manuel on whose land they worked. They did not like to contradict Señor Rivera who gave them credit at his store. Although many of the *campesinos* were reluctant to speak now, they agreed with Edmundo who seemed to speak for them.

"So you see, *maestro*," Edmundo was saying, "we wish to make known our needs to the officials in the Ministry of Education in Lima, but the people here are afraid."

"Yes," said the teacher, "I know."

"We cannot ask for another teacher and a larger school if our own village leaders do not wish it. And we who work on other men's land depend upon the good will of the owners. We dare not disagree or quarrel with them, or our families will suffer."

"And so," said Señor Valdez, "you wish me to speak for you to obtain their agreement?"

"Yes, Señor Valdez, and then we could send all our names to Lima. We could build a great school here. We could make . . ."

"Yes," interrupted the teacher, "but what if I, too, should be fearful of the landowner and the alcalde and the storekeeper? What then?"

"Ohhhh . . ." Then silence.

"Are you, Señor Valdez? Are you also afraid?" whispered Carlos.

"Well," replied the teacher, "I could be sent to another village, to Curahuasi, for example, or even to Oxapampa, in the *montaña*. And I am so fond of Urubamba and its people."

"No, men," he continued, "if I have one small bit of learning, it is that fear has no place among us. We are right in our requests. I shall speak to the noble leaders of our town, and we *shall* have a school!"

And he looked at Carlos and smiled.

So it turned out that Señor Valdez spoke plainly, and

as an equal, to the alcalde, to the storekeeper, and to the owner of the great *hacienda,* Don Manuel.

He talked with each separately and explained how with better education men were better workers. They understood more and could take greater responsibilities. They cared better for themselves and their families, so that people were healthier.

He described how the children of the poor could become better farmers, but they could also be teachers and engineers and highly skilled workers of all kinds.

Listening to this, Don Manuel protested.

"My *campesinos* have always done well on my land. I have lived close to them and have helped them in the bad years. This I shall always do. But I see no reason why their children need as good an education as mine. They are, after all, primitive people, and even your school is more than they really need."

As for the alcalde, he had been persuaded by his friends that there was no need for more schooling.

"These people," he said, "are like children. They know that we will always look after them. You tell them they can always come to me if they feel that Don Manuel or Señor Rivera is neglecting them. Now, go, and don't be stirring them up!"

Señor Rivera listened carefully to the teacher's explanation. "So," he said, "you feel that another class and a teacher would be good for Urubamba? Would it also increase trade in my store? Would people who are learning want more kerosine and lamps? Would they want more paper and pencils?"

"Yes," replied the teacher vigorously. "I am sure of it!"

"Well," answered the storekeeper slowly, "and so what is your plan?"

"We will write our petition to the Minister of Education, with the names of all of our *padres de familias,* the fathers of schoolchildren. And we would promise to build a second schoolroom ourselves, if the officials in Lima will send a teacher for the last two grades. I know we will be given what we ask . . ."

"You know," interrupted Señor Rivera, "and I suppose you will want my name on your petition also?"

"Of course, as one of the leading men of Urubamba your name should lead the others."

"Hmmm. We shall see . . ." was the slow reply of the storekeeper. "We shall see."

That evening, by the light of his lamp, the teacher labored over a petition to the Minister of Education in Lima. He wrote clearly and simply that the town of Urubamba would build a school for the full six-year primary program. Would the ministry send a second teacher?

It was a plain statement, respectfully addressed and submitted. There was plenty of space below the letter and on the back of it for signatures.

And, he thought, there must be space also for thumbprints. For the law said that a man who could not write his name, might put his thumbprint on the page and a scribe could write his name for him under it. There would be many thumbprints on this petition.

4

THE NEXT FEW DAYS WERE BUSY AND EXCITING FOR ALL THE men and for some of the boys, including Carlos. Wherever Edmundo went he, too, had gone. He had listened carefully to all the questions and the arguments.

Some of the young men had been very eager to have the petitions signed and had been too stern with their neighbors, insisting that they sign. Explanations were not really important, they had said.

"We know it is right, therefore you must sign!"

"No, no," said a few of the *taitas, padres de familias.* "I am not ready to sign something I don't understand. And no young fledgling will make me do it!"

Others had said, "I dare not." And not a word more.

But most of the people of the town and the valley were ready to sign. They were fearful, but they were not alone. Surely they would not be put off the land for wanting more learning for their children!

And the pages grew in number with all the names and thumbprints under them.

Carlos listened to all the arguments and heard the anger and the enthusiasm of the young men. His eyes glistened and danced as he helped at the teacher's house one evening.

"Now, Señor Valdez," Edmundo was saying, "don't

you think we have enough signatures? Why not send the petitions to Lima right away?"

The teacher slowly shook his head. "With all these signatures, we must still say 'maybe.'"

"But why, *maestro*," whispered Carlos, "what more is needed?"

Señor Valdez looked around the room at the others, who had worked so hard and wanted so much to see the results of their work.

"We still need at least three more signatures," he said.

The men were puzzled. They looked at one another, thinking how strange the teacher seemed now.

Edmundo was about to speak, to ask another question, when suddenly the door opened. Padre Manya stood on the threshold.

The priest was a young man, a *cholo* in appearance like the others, but his black robe and round collar gave him a very serious, dignified look. He was loved and respected in his village for his kindness and interest in everyone.

He turned to the teacher and asked him what was new. Señor Valdez smiled and, instead of answering the priest, asked his own question.

"May I ask why the padre has been so long away from us? What duties did he have to undertake in the city?"

His eyes twinkled as he spoke to his friend.

"In Cuzco," said Padre Manya, "I learned many things. I learned that there has been a new school built in Urubamba and that all the children are now able to attend. I found out that there are now two teachers instead of only one. And, in addition to all this, I discovered that Don Manuel, Señor Rivera, and the alcalde had contributed the furniture for the new classroom."

Señor Valdez laughed aloud at this story and said, "I

see they are talking about us in Cuzco. Is it that important, do you think?"

"Yes, my friends," said the priest, as he looked at the men in the room. "People from other villages are interested in what you are trying to do. They hope that you will succeed so that they may do something for better education in their towns."

"Padre," shouted Edmundo, "see how we have gathered the signatures of our people here! We are ready to send our petition to Lima, but Señor Valdez continues to say we are not ready."

"But we . . ." The men heard that word, "we," with a strange excitement. "We are not ready unless we get at least three more of our neighbors to sign."

"Padre, what do you mean? Señor Valdez has said the same thing."

"Don't you know," replied Padre Manya, "that we cannot send this petition until we have the names of Don Manuel, Señor Rivera, and the alcalde?"

A silence fell upon the room. Carlos blinked his eyes, not understanding. This was an impossible task, and their plans were doomed!

"Without the leaders of our community, our petition is not enough. The men who are educated, who have responsibilities in the town, must also see that our needs for schooling are important. Even our hundreds of signatures mean little if we are not all together."

"But," wailed Carlos, "they will never sign a petition for another school and a teacher!"

"Ah," said Padre Manya, "they will, and I shall see that they do."

The men left the teacher's house a short time later, shaking their heads.

"Do you think the padre will succeed?"

"If the padre says so, it will be so!"

As Carlos went to the door, Padre Manya beckoned to him. He turned to the priest and listened respectfully.

"Carlito," said Padre Manya, "I have other news from Cuzco. There is a job which will take you to Lima. Come and see me tomorrow."

Carlos stared.

"Hasta mañana," said Padre Manya.

The next morning Carlos didn't notice if it was raining or if the sun shone. What he saw was the road past the house leading to the village. In the plaza was the little church which had stood there for many years. And, walking with dignity but not calm, Carlos held his head high as he entered the church.

He held his *chullo* clutched in his hands while his eyes grew accustomed to the dim light. There, in front of the altar, was the padre, kneeling, his eyes closed, hands clasped, in the faint rays of a few flickering candles.

Carlos knelt swiftly, then he came softly to the side altar. He held a crude new candle which his *abuelita* had given him.

As the light grew brighter for a moment, Padre Manya opened his eyes and saw Carlos. He gazed once toward the altar and made the sign of the cross. Then, rising, he beckoned to Carlos and they went to his little room at the back of the church.

"I said there was a job for you, Carlito. One that would take you to Lima. Would that be to your liking?"

Carlos' lips were dry. His tongue was dry in his mouth. But he nodded his head eagerly and then at last he could say, "Oh, yes, Padre!"

"Well, my son. You must be in Cuzco tomorrow afternoon. There, near the Plaza de Armas you will find the bus, *El Cóndor Dorado*. If you look just a moment, you will find the *piloto*, Don Vicente. He is my friend of many years.

You will give him this note and tell Don Vicente that you hope to be his helper, his *chulillo*. And then he will tell you what to do. I have talked with your father. Soon you will be on your way to Lima."

Carlos nodded his head up and down, then looked at Padre Manya. There might be more to know.

The priest stood up and touched the boy on the shoulder. He handed him a letter.

"Go now, my son," he said. "You are strong and you

have courage. You have learned something in your few years. Don Vicente will make a *chulillo* of you. Perhaps you may someday be a *piloto* yourself."

He paused, then gently placed his hand on the boy's head. He murmured words of blessing.

Carlos could only mumble a faint "Thank you, Padre," and then quickly, he ran for the door. This time, too, he thought of his dignity, but it lasted for only a short distance. Carlos ran, almost flew, to the road, down the old Inca highway, away from the town, toward his house.

When he entered the adobe hut, he was about to burst with the news.

"Father!" he called. "Mother! 'Mundo! *Abuelita!* Come and listen!"

The work in the little house stopped as heads turned toward Carlos. Even Martita, whom he had left out, dropped her broom of twigs and came in from the yard.

Carlos told his good news, and his brother smiled. His father, too, seemed pleased at the happiness his son now showed. He and Edmundo had agreed that Carlos should have this chance to try himself out. But the women only sighed.

As if in chorus, his mother and grandmother both saw another side to his good fortune.

"You will leave us and go into the Lord knows what dangers," worried his mother.

". . . what dangers!" echoed his grandmother.

"And you are so young, how will you know enough to take care of yourself?" said his mother.

". . . take care of yourself!" moaned his grandmother.

But Carlos could only answer that here, at last, was his best dream come true. "A job! A bus helper—a *chulillo!* A *copiloto,* practically!"

Edmundo shook his head and said seriously, "No, Carlito, not nearly a *copiloto,* but . . ." He was about to say more, but a glance at his father told him when to be silent.

And so, his last day at home, Carlos planned his farewells. He would go to visit some of his friends. He would stop at the adobe hut where his friend Ricardo's parents lived. They would give him the address of their son in Lima.

Of course, he was going to say goodbye to Señor Valdez, who was his special friend and who had taught him so much.

In the dark little schoolroom where he had sat for four years, Carlos now faced Señor Valdez alone.

"Tell me, Carlito," said the teacher, "are you not afraid to go away from home, from our Urubamba?"

"*Ay*, Señor Valdez, you know how I have dreamed of being a man and of working. So many times when you spoke to us of the great ocean, of the beautiful Lima, I wished to see them for myself. No, how could I be afraid?"

"Good boy," replied the teacher. "But I must give you some advice. Be a *little* afraid. It will make you thoughtful and cautious. Fear to act in haste, or in anger. Fear what you do not know or understand, but do not turn your back on knowing and understanding."

"Yes, sir," said Carlos.

"There is so much to remind you and to warn you about. But if I packed your mind with warning, would you have room for questions?"

The teacher sat thoughtfully for a moment. Then, turning his face toward Carlos, he said with a smile, "You are a good boy and shall be a fine young man. We shall be proud of you, Carlito. Go with God!"

Then, with a firm handshake and the touch of the teacher on his shoulder, Carlos strode out of the school.

Later that night, under the bright stars and a slender crescent moon, Carlos, Edmundo, and their father sat staring into the embers of a small fire.

The women of the family had been busy all day, mending, cutting dried meat, and preparing the *chuño,* the tiny potatoes that are left to freeze in the fields. They were gathering what they could for Carlos' bundle tomorrow.

Outside, Edmundo spoke softly and told of adventures on Peru's highways. He told of the dust that coats the teeth and mouth and enters the nose. He described the ruts and tracks which held the buses and trucks, but which rattled the bones, especially of the *chulillo.*

Dangers there were, of careless drivers, tired or ill or drunken. He mentioned the dangers of floods and landslides, when trucks tumbled like toys into deep canyons.

"Adventure you may have, Carlito," said Edmundo earnestly, "but see to it that you take care of yourself."

"Ay," nodded Señor Bernal, their father, "we cannot keep our eagle at home, but we want him to fly back to us."

"Yes, *taita,*" replied Carlos, "I will do my best."

That night, as the stars made their endless circles, Carlos dreamed of thunder and lightning in the Andes. He saw the narrow Inca roads that led to the lower valleys and finally to the sea. In his dream, the wind snatched at him and his tasseled cap as he rode on the top of the *Cóndor Dorado* all the way to Lima.

5

THE ROAD TO CUZCO WAS A ROCKY, DUSTY TRAIL. It followed the bed of the ancient Inca highway of centuries ago. Alongside ran the cold, clear Urubamba River, finding its way as the Vilcanota, then as the Ucayali, to the mighty Amazon.

As the dust rose and the pebbles flew, Carlos and his family rode in the back of a truck eagerly watching for signs of Cuzco.

For Carlos, standing beside Edmundo, all that mattered was the end of the road, Cuzco. The *Cóndor Dorado* would be standing in the plaza, shiny and new, waiting for its *chulillo*. Don Vicente would be another teacher, happy and cheerful, whose sure hand would soon take them to Lima.

The road wound slowly past ruins of ancient fortresses, past the huge boulders of Sacsahuaman, and then it coiled itself around Cuzco. It slid past adobe houses with red tile roofs, over cobblestone streets. There were churches and stores, a movie house, the hotel, and at last, the Plaza de Armas. The truck stopped.

Impatiently, Carlos waited for his family to leave the truck. He looked around the plaza and saw four or five drab buses in a line at the side of the small hotel.

There! There it was! The *Cóndor Dorado!* It was a sturdy-looking bus, painted a faded yellow, coated with dust. Over the front windshield, on a blue board, were the words EL CÓNDOR DORADO.

Carlos and Edmundo stopped and looked thoughtfully at the bus. Carlos read the letters on the sign and then peeked in through the open door. Edmundo walked around the bus and looked at the tires. He stooped down to study the underbody, the springs, and the axles.

The rest of the family stood silently at a respectful distance, waiting.

Suddenly, a hoarse voice came from the hotel doorway.

"Well . . . if it suits you, will you ride to Lima with her? Or would you like to buy her, maybe?"

Carlos looked up, startled. Edmundo came around to the sidewalk.

"Don Vicente?" he asked calmly.

"Well, señorito, and what if I am?"

They saw a short stocky man in shirt-sleeves and city clothes who came up from the bench in the doorway. He walked scowling toward Edmundo. With his hands on his hips, he faced the young man and waited.

Carlos spoke up quickly, saying, "Señor Don Vicente, I have a letter for you from Padre Manya of Urubamba who is our friend."

Quickly, Don Vicente took the letter, and as he read it, he looked at Carlos from time to time. His bushy eyebrows went up and down, his nose wrinkled, but he said nothing as he read to the end.

At last he turned to Edmundo and said softly, "So this one wants to be a *chulillo?* He wants to work for me?"

"Yes, Don Vicente," said Edmundo, "I think he will do well. He is clever and strong."

"But why does the padre send him to me?" he grumbled. "What does he know of this work? To be a *chulillo* on a bus is not child's play!"

"Señor," replied Edmundo, "he knows of these things.

He has heard much of the tasks on the highway. I have told him of the dangers and the hardships. And still he wants to work for you and go to Lima."

The *piloto* looked over the young Indian farmer.

"You have told him!" he said scornfully. "What can you know of this?"

"Do you know Florencio Reyes, Don Vicente?"

"Of course! I know he has been a great driver on the worst highways. I know of his strength and his skill with the heavy trucks."

"He was my *copiloto*," replied Edmundo. "I took him as my *chulillo* when he first started to work."

"Ah!" whispered Don Vicente, "so you are Don Edmundo Bernal, of whom he has spoken! I know of you too, then, señor."

Saying this, he put out his hand and grasped Edmundo's. He turned to Carlos.

"So, your brother is one of us! A fine man!"

Don Vicente took the priest's letter and reread it. He looked Carlos over again, but this time, his eyebrows remained still and his nose did not wrinkle.

"Padre Manya is an old friend. I am glad he has sent you to me."

"You are kind to take on this young one," answered Edmundo, "but he will work well."

Carlos nodded his head vigorously.

"All right!" said Don Vicente. "Let's see about his work. You get him started with the loading, while I go and round up my passengers. We leave in an hour!"

With that, he went back into the hotel, and his voice could be heard calling hoarsely as he went, *"Cóndor Dorado . . . for Lima! Cóndor Dorado! . . . "*

Then, as the family watched, Edmundo had Carlos sling his sack into the bus beside the driver's seat. He showed the boy how to climb the slender steel ladder up the back of the bus. He explained how the cargo nets must be spread to hold the luggage and boxes and sacks which travelers carry in Peru.

Together they found where Don Vicente kept his tools for making repairs on the bus. Edmundo was glad to see that Don Vicente was also one of the unusual drivers who kept a lantern, two shovels, and some extra blankets in his case under the rear seats.

This was a *piloto,* for sure, thought Edmundo, as he helped Carlos with the loading. But there was so much more he wanted to tell his young brother. About how to be a *chulillo* who did not anger his master, and who did not lose any cargo, and who did not, in the weary hours of riding, lose his hold or his balance and fall. But the time had passed for such lessons. . . .

For Carlos, all went quickly. Passengers came and entered the *Cóndor Dorado.* There were old men, going to Lima to visit children. There were women with bright-eyed babies slung over their shoulders in colorful shawls. Some families were going to Lima with their children, all fearful of the noisy unfamiliar crowd. They were reluctant to give up their thin suitcases and bundles, and they held tightly to their sacks.

The bus soon filled, and Don Vicente climbed up to the roof where Carlos was tying down the cargo nets. He growled his approval and then went down into the bus to be sure all fares were paid.

Carlos came to stand by his family, and for the first time in years, he took his mother's hand. He embraced his grandmother and his tearful sister. Then, as the motor of the *Cóndor Dorado* roared, Carlos quickly embraced his father and his brother. He felt a sudden sharp pang of fear, and for one brief moment, he wanted to stay close within the warmth of his family.

Then the motor roared again, and he felt a pressure from his father's hand. And with his brother's firm grip on his arm, he climbed up the ladder of the bus.

Slowly, the *Cóndor Dorado* pulled away from the plaza, and Carlos waved to his family. The wind snatched at his tasseled cap as the bus took the road to Lima.

Carlos, holding tightly to the cargo net, sprawled on the top of the bus, and dreamed of what was before him. Already he imagined the towers of Lima and the busy crowds of people. But even more, he could see his friend Ricardo, with whom he could talk over the time they had missed since school closed. Ricardo was already a city boy, thought Carlos, and would have many adventures to tell about.

For many hours, Carlos clung to the bus, sometimes on his back, sometimes on his stomach. From time to time, while there was still light, he saw a soaring condor drifting lazily above the land. He saw the blue-gray smoke from the huts of *campesinos* like his own father.

The bus rocked, it creaked, it shook him on the roof, sometimes gently, sometimes with violence. But Carlos held on, and as the sun went down in the west, beyond the mountains, he began to feel the bite of the cold wind. He wrapped his wool scarf more tightly over his face to keep the dust out and to feel the warmth of his own breath.

Don Vicente was now driving more slowly. As he came to curves in the narrow road, he sounded the horn loudly and with pride for the *Cóndor Dorado*. Carlos crept forward to the edge of the bus roof. He knew that he must now watch carefully for dangers in the road.

In the half-light, a flock of sheep or a herd of llamas was not so easy for a driver to see. The *chulillo* on the roof of the bus could see farther and more clearly over the dust of the road. Carlos peered ahead, blinking his eyes to ease them. He looked for the lights of approaching trucks or buses. He looked for the small red taillights of slower-moving traffic.

Now more than ever, Don Vicente and his passengers were depending upon Carlos' sharp eyes and his keen ears.

There! A moving light . . . a pair! Carlos leaned forward to rap the windshield in front of Don Vicente. He pointed forward and shouted into the wind. Don Vicente could hear nothing, but he slowed the bus even more and began to blink his lights and to sound his horn.

Coming nearer and nearer, the other driver kept his pace and did not blink his lights at all. Carlos grew worried and he rapped harder on the windshield. His *piloto* slowly pulled the bus over to a narrow ledge on the side of the road against the mountain. He kept his lights switching on and off as Carlos waited anxiously above.

Still closer came the lights. It was almost dark now. Carlos stood up tall on the roof and wanted to shout, but it would not have mattered. The other driver would never hear him over the sound of his own engine.

Then, coming around the last curve in the narrow, winding road, the headlights began to blink and they heard the engine labor more and more slowly. Don Vicente had tried to leave room to pass, but on this narrow road it meant a careful, slow drive along the edge of a sharp drop to the river below.

At last, Carlos saw a small truck, with a flatbed and stakes, coming up to them. The driver stopped his truck, and they could see about twenty people, standing close together in silence, on the flatbed holding onto the stakes.

"Ho!" shouted Don Vicente, "I think you can get by. I have left room for your toy to pass!"

"Señor," replied the other driver respectfully, "with my people, I am not sure. We may be too heavy for the shoulder

of this road, and I do not like the sounds of the water down there!"

"Well," answered Don Vicente from his window, "I will try to come closer to the mountain, but your people must get off, or you will have them in the river with you."

As they watched, the skillful driver moved his bus back down the road. Carlos signaled from above and shouted for him to come still closer to the mountain. Carlos climbed down the ladder of the *Cóndor* and went to help open the tailgate of the truck. The people were like himself, men, women, and children of the nearby towns. They carried their belongings in sacks, and silently they let him help them down from the truck.

Carlos reached up for little girls like his own sister, Martita, to lift them down onto the dusty road. Spry boys like himself, and older ones, clambered briskly down and stood beside their parents.

Then, when all were on the road, they shouldered their sacks and their bundles, as the truck slowly moved forward, nearly brushing the bus as it passed. When the driver had gone beyond the *Cóndor,* he stopped his truck and the people moved forward to take their places on the flatbed once more.

When they had returned to the truck, Carlos walked back to the *Cóndor* where Don Vicente and the truck driver were talking.

"Has there been rain?" Don Vicente was asking.

"Yes, *maestro,*" replied the other, "just beyond Abancay, within twenty kilometers there was rain.

"But," he added, "the road is packed hard and the traffic is light. It should be no problem for you."

"Yes," said Don Vicente, "no problem for me if I keep to the center of the road, and if your friends who drive trucks will watch as well as my boy here."

Carlos felt a thrill of satisfaction. He knew he had

done well, and this was Don Vicente's way of praising him. After all, this was his job and he knew what he must do.

The other driver had no reply for the light scolding, and Don Vicente beckoned Carlos, moving his head toward the rear of the *Cóndor*.

"Up you go, Carlito," was the signal he gave.

Carlos ran for the ladder, glad for the chance to stretch and walk, and even more glad to show what a fine *chulillo* he was.

On the roof, Carlos stretched out on his stomach, peering ahead for glimpses of other lights or for the sound of other engines. As he felt the rhythm of the wheels on the road below, he felt his strength and that of Don Vicente in the driver's seat, while above, the sprinkling of stars gave them nothing to worry about.

In a few hours, the *Cóndor* reached Abancay and Don Vicente drove along the cobbled streets until he found his station in the town square. He stopped the bus alongside the high curb of the plaza and reminded his passengers that they would find food and rest here. Tomorrow they would drive on an hour after dawn.

"Ay, Carlito," yawned the driver, "stay now and help unload for those who wish their bundles. I'm off to get a hot meal."

Weary as he was, Carlos climbed up to the roof and pulled the cargo net aside. He watched Don Vicente disappear into the restaurant opposite them, and already the warm, spicy cooking odors reached his nostrils.

Ay! he thought, how hungry I am! And I must stay and work for who knows how long.

In a very short time, the bundles had been sorted out. Slowly the passengers drifted away to find a meal or to seek lodgings for the night.

Then Carlos, with nothing to do, went down to the

bus and got his own bundle. From it he took his warm poncho and another cap. Wrapping himself in his clothing, he closed the door of the bus and stretched across the rear seat to wait for his master, Don Vicente.

Carlos closed his eyes and heard the sounds of people close by. Farther off were the sounds of music. He could only see the single street light of the plaza, and all the sounds were mingled as he quickly fell asleep.

In what seemed like only a few minutes, Carlos awoke with a start. He heard a pounding on the door of the bus and a loud voice calling.

"Carlos! Carlos!" Don Vicente was shouting. "You silly boy, let me in!"

He sprang to open the door and saw that his *piloto* was carrying buckets of food and a small loaf of bread.

He smiled. "Here I am, *maestro*."

"Well, boy," said Don Vicente, "do your bones ache now?"

"They are well, *maestro*."

"And your ears," continued the *piloto*, "don't you hear the whistling of the wind?"

"Not any more, Don Vicente."

"Well, then I am sure," he went on with a grin, "that your empty stomach is no longer rumbling."

"Oh no." Carlos smiled weakly. "It rumbles mightily."

With that, Don Vicente roared with laughter and held out the stacked buckets and the bread.

As Carlos ate greedily, his master waved his hand and left the bus.

"Sleep well, boy!" he called, "I'll see you at dawn. We will have much work to do then. And if you need me, call loudly. I am just within the house here."

Alone again, Carlos set the buckets aside. He looked

out at the town with its shadows and mingled noises. Stretching himself out again, he winked at a star, and then was asleep, to dream of a rolling, bumping bus on the road to Lima.

6

A SHARP SLAP ON THE DOOR MADE HIM SPRING SUDDENLY awake. There was Don Vicente, waiting to come into the bus, and he had said there was work to be done.

"*Maestro,*" muttered Carlos, "*buenos días.*"

Don Vicente looked at him sharply. He started to speak, but for just a moment he realized that yesterday was his helper's first day of work.

"Go, boy," he said, "go out to the house there. They will give you something hot to start the day. But do not waste time. I need you right away."

"Yes, *maestro,*" answered Carlos, with more energy than before.

In the house he found an *abuelita* much like his own grandmother, who gave him a pitcher of water and told him to wash in the courtyard. Then she set before him on a wooden table a bowl of porridge and a hard roll. She asked if he wanted tea, but Carlos did not wish to be too long, so he politely refused.

In a short time, he returned to the *Cóndor* and found that the *piloto* had opened the hood of the engine. He was studying the inside thoughtfully.

When he saw Carlos, he said, "Quickly now, Carlos, you must sweep out the bus. Then I want the windshield washed, and then all the other windows."

Carlos went to work immediately and the dust of yesterday's travel began to fly. Don Vicente watched him only once in a while, but he could see that Carlos was doing as he was told.

Here is a boy, he thought, who works with a good heart.

Then, as the sun rose higher and the day became lighter, Carlos could see that the bus looked more brown than yellow.

"*Maestro*," he asked, "shall I wash the bus on all sides, also?"

"No," replied the driver. "That we shall do tomorrow, but be sure to look up above at the cargo net. The passengers are beginning to return."

Carlos climbed quickly up the ladder and prepared to receive the bundles as the passengers handed them up. He smiled at them as they greeted him this morning.

"*Hola, chico!*" called a chunky little man, who passed a suitcase up to the roof.

"Señor," replied Carlos.

He smiled to see some of the families as they went back into the bus, children still chewing their hard rolls, mothers directing where each one would sit today.

One man stood below and argued with Don Vicente about a crate of chickens he had bought.

"No!" shouted the driver, "chickens do not ride in the *Cóndor!* They ride above with my *chulillo!*"

"But, *maestro*," argued the man, "they will die in the wind up there. And besides, I have paid my fare to Nazca. You cannot refuse my baggage. I shall complain to the *guardia civil!*"

"Oh, you're going to the *guardia* about these chickens? We'll see about it."

Don Vicente barred the door to the bus. The other passengers, those inside and those waiting to enter, joined in the argument.

The driver was stubborn. He insisted that he didn't have to carry chickens inside his bus. They were dirty and noisy, and they smelled. No more was to be said. He folded his arms.

"The driver is right!" shouted one of the passengers. "You can send the chickens to the roof. We don't want to wait any longer for you."

"Yes, make up your mind," said another, while Don Vicente stood with folded arms.

At last, wearily, the man said, "All right, I'll give them to the boy up there. But you will be responsible for them!"

Don Vicente broke into a smile.

"Not only will I be responsible, but also Carlos there, who is the best *chulillo* in all of the south of Peru. He will be most careful and responsible."

Then, looking up at Carlos, he said, "And see that every one of those birds is still clucking when we reach Nazca!"

So Carlos placed the crate carefully and planned to shield the chickens against the wind when the bus started.

They were on their way, and the *Cóndor* rolled steadily over the bumpy, rutted mountain road. Carlos clung to the top and watched for trouble up ahead. He had placed some suitcases and canvas as a windshield for the chickens, and they rode placidly along with him.

Never worried, but always alert, Don Vicente handled the bus with respect. He did not take needless risks or drive it under strain. Nor did he let the bus drive him, gaining speed and crowding other drivers to pass. Don Vicente knew that all his passengers had confidence in him. Carlos now understood what Edmundo had meant when he said Don Vicente was a fine *piloto*.

As the road rushed by, they noticed the little shrines near the edge of the highway from time to time. Sometimes there was a simple block of stone surmounted by a cross, with a few flowers. And sometimes the shrine had a small image or a statue. Carlos knew that each of these was a roadside reminder of an accident in which people had been hurt or killed. Looking over the edge of the road, he sometimes saw bits of wreckage that had been left below. But with each cross, Carlos thought of his own *piloto,* driving steadily and with care.

Suddenly, as Carlos watched, he saw a man in the road, waving his hand at them, shouting, just before they came to a curve. He leaned forward to pound on the window above the driver, when he felt the bus slowing down. Don Vicente had seen the man, too, and was stopping the bus.

"Slowly! Slowly!" the man called.

"What is the matter, man?" called Don Vicente in his most irritated manner. He was very anxious not to lose time on the way to Lima. Behind him in the bus, the passengers murmured and rustled, worried about the sudden halt in their journey.

"You must stop, *maestro,*" called the man. "The road ahead is blocked. You cannot go forward—not even for the love of the saints!"

"*Caray!*" muttered Don Vicente, "what a time for a landslide!"

Then, with great caution, he maneuvered the bus slowly forward around the curve in the road where they could see what was wrong.

Carlos blinked and wiped the dust from his face. Ahead of the *Cóndor* were three other buses and a truck halted in the middle of the road. The road itself looked as if it ran right into the side of a mountain, and there it stopped.

Don Vicente called up to his *chulillo.* "Carlito, get down here right away, and we'll have a look around!"

Some of the passengers began to get up from their seats when the driver said reassuringly, "Don't you worry. Stretch your legs and be comfortable. I have seen such landslides before, and with the Lord's help and a few strong backs, we shall soon be on our way again."

Then he and Carlos walked forward to a group of drivers and boys who stood at the foot of the small mountain which now covered the road.

Greetings were exchanged among old friends and fellow drivers, and then Don Vicente asked for information.

"Well," he asked, "is this a few hours' work, or do we form a colony and settle here?"

"Ay, Vicente," grinned another driver, "one of the boys has climbed over this hill, and it is no easy task we have."

"What do you think?" he asked another.

"We have sent some of the boys ahead to find the *campesinos* who work in the fields above here. They should return soon. And since we aren't far from Curahuasi, we may have the help of the army garrison there. I think we may be resting here for a couple of days at the most."

"Ay!" shouted Don Vicente, and he clasped his head with both hands. "This miserable road! I shall report it once more to the ministry officials in Lima!"

"Yes, Vicente," answered one of the other drivers. "You can report it for all of us—if you ever get there!"

"I'll get there," growled Don Vicente, "but let's see what we can do about it now!"

And with that, he told Carlos to bring out the shovel from the *Cóndor*. He asked which of the others also carried shovels or any kinds of digging tools.

Don Vicente was a man who hated to be idle when he could organize people for a job. He had Carlos and the three other *chulillos* digging into the mountain that blocked the road. As they dug, some of the passengers who had come up from the buses also carried huge stones away to the edge of the road and dumped them down to the river below.

Women passengers sat with their children now alongside the buses and fed the littlest ones. The older children wandered about, exploring the steep sides of the road or teetering dangerously near the edge above the river. Worried mothers called out. Children played or helped carry stones. The older people walked slowly in and out of the buses, or rested comfortably in the cool seats.

Lucky for us, thought Carlos as he dug his shovel into the rocky soil, that we have no more rain.

He looked up at the clear sky and wished that the soldiers from Curahuasi would get there soon.

Don Vicente had told him to work at the mass of earth and to keep right on digging. Now, as it grew darker, he felt hungry and his very bones were weary.

A few at a time, the *chulillos* and the other helpers drifted away to their own vehicles. Kerosine lamps were lit in one or two places, and small fires were built at the side of the road. The drivers had agreed that cooking could be done in one area only. It had to be well away from the trucks and buses. A few people had made the dangerous trip down the steep mountainside to the river for water.

In the *Cóndor,* Don Vicente sat strangely silent. He looked around at his passengers who sat in their seats or clustered in groups outside the bus.

"Carlos!" he called, and beckoned to the boy to come into the bus beside him.

"*Hombre,*" he said, "you have worked enough for today. It's time to eat and rest."

Don Vicente held out a piece of dried meat, and there were a few bits of *chuño,* the frozen potato, that he had brought from home.

"And when you pray tonight," said the driver, "be sure

you pray that the army will send men and machines to clear the road—and that it will not rain before they arrive!"

The day was announced by the roosters crowing on the roof of the *Cóndor*. It was greeted by squalling babies whose mothers hastened to take them to their breasts to be fed. As the babies grew still, Carlos knew he had to get up from under his poncho.

How his bones ached! And yet there was the mountain of earth, covering the road, and there were the *pilotos,* urging the boys to finish their morning tea and bread.

"Come now!" they called. "Let's get on with the work!"

Carlos went to dig, already feeling tired. At his side was another *chulillo,* also working away at the hill.

"Ay!" moaned the boy. "For this I had to leave my mother in Lima!"

And he threw a shovelful of earth to the side of the road.

"For this I had to give up shining shoes in the Plaza de Armas!"

Another shovel of earth flew by.

"*Caray!* When will I see Miraflores again?"

His voice nearly broke with the sound of his grief.

Carlos dug silently. As he worked, he cast glances at this companion. He had heard the almost-tearful complaints, but there was nothing he wanted to say. He just listened for more.

"Well, *campesino,*" said the boy next to him. "You're not new at this kind of work, are you?"

"I am no *campesino,*" Carlos answered softly, "but my parents and brother work the land. Our fields are near Urubamba."

"I know how it is," said the boy. "My family used to work on the land, but that was long ago. We are all *Limeños* now, and I shall someday have my own truck."

He spoke almost defiantly, as if he expected an argument over his future plans.

Then, reaching his hand to Carlos, he said, "Look, my name is Pablo, and I like the way you work. I meant no offense to you."

"I know," replied Carlos. "This is my first trip, Pablo. We are driving the *Cóndor Dorado,* Don Vicente and I. Carlos is my name."

They smiled at one another and went on with the digging. On all sides, people dug at the mountain which still blocked the road.

Pablo and Carlos found the time to talk about many things. Carlos discovered that Pablo and his family lived in Lima, but he had never been to school there. As long as he could remember, Pablo had worked at running errands, shining shoes, carrying boxes, or doing anything that he and his older brothers could find.

His mother also worked as she could, to keep their tin-roofed shack clean and to prepare the rice or the beans that they could afford. Sometimes there was a piece of fish, a reward for a day's errands.

Pablo knew Lima well, and for Carlos' benefit, he described the clang and rattle of the streetcars as they rumbled through the busy streets. He closed his eyes as he told about the fish sellers in the *mercados,* the *anticucho* broilers, the docksides at Callao, and the airport. All Lima was his, said Pablo, and he couldn't wait to get there.

He grinned and said how tired he was getting of this "miserable" shovel. Carlos nodded in agreement, and as they dug, they both wished they were back on top of a bus, rocking and clinging in the dust of the road.

As the day wore on, the landslide was attacked by bus helpers, passengers, and even by some of the children. All this work was done in spurts, and the people stopped often. Now there was *chicha,* the corn beer, being poured, and the laughter was growing louder while the work grew less.

Once, when Carlos went back to the *Cóndor* to rest, he saw Don Vicente in serious conversation with two other drivers. It was not his place to listen, so he crawled in and stretched across two seats. Still, he felt the men were worried, and he knew they were going to have to think about turning back. It would then be a profitless trip, indeed. Worst of all, Carlos would be as far from Lima as ever. What would he do then?

It was nearly nightfall when he awoke, and Don Vicente was nowhere in sight. There was a great deal of shouting going on, and he clambered out of the bus, rubbing his eyes. Then he saw at a distance, in the middle of the blocked road, Don Vicente and the other drivers standing with two strangers.

The men were telling the drivers that a group of nearby villagers would come tomorrow to help with the work of clearing the road. Besides, they said, word had been sent to the army post at Curahuasi for soldiers and machines.

Soldiers were very good at this kind of work and had much experience on the roads all over Peru. But, they added with caution, since this was a matter of the army, no one could say for sure when they would arrive.

The next day, Carlos and Pablo stood together near the side of the road and watched as the two dozen farmers worked steadily at the slide that still blocked the road.

"Well, Carlos," grinned Pablo, "there you see people who know how to solve problems. What luck that so many could come!"

"Yes," said Carlos without a smile. "They could be working on their own lands and solving their own problems. What luck for us!"

Carlos saw the quiet manner and the unsmiling goodwill of these men, and he saw his father, with Edmundo and himself, clearing their land and often that of others who were in need. And besides this, they had to work the land of the *hacendado* for their wages and share of the crop. Watching their faces and their working ways, Carlos remembered.

As the digging continued, there was more time for Carlos to wander with Pablo and to talk with some of the other *chulillos*. And while Carlos spent time with the other boys, Don Vicente was able to meet with the other drivers. It was not often that they could get together this way outside the plaza in Lima.

Later, while Carlos was sitting around a small fire by the side of the road with several of the other *chulillos*, a small boy came up to the group and tugged at his sleeve.

"Yes, *chico*," said Carlos, "what it it?"

"Señor Carlos," said the little one, "Don Vicente wants you right away."

Carlos stood up promptly and, while the other boys winked at each other and jeered at him for obeying so quickly, he nodded at Pablo and went to find Don Vicente.

The driver was sitting inside the *Cóndor* and, when Carlos walked up, he smiled.

"I am glad you didn't make me wait for you," he said. "Too many *chulillos* fail to please their masters."

"Yes, sir," said Carlos respectfully.

"I want you to start washing and cleaning the *Cóndor*, inside and out. I'm going to work on the engine and make sure we can reach Lima with no difficulties. There are rags behind the rear seat, and you know where the water is."

Carlos went to work. He had to make his way with his buckets down to the river. He had to clear the cargo completely off the roof of the *Cóndor* and then return it in good order. The job was difficult, especially with the chickens, but when he was through the bus would shine.

He was glad to be working on the *Cóndor* again, and almost side by side with his *piloto*. He noticed that after he and Don Vicente started to work, several of the other drivers and their helpers began to do the same.

While Carlos washed and wiped and swept, he saw that his driver had taken a number of parts out of the engine and carefully laid them on a mat by the side of the bus. He hoped that some day soon he could learn about the engine, too, and about what made the bus go. He knew already that being a driver was not enough. One must also know what one was driving and how to keep it in good condition.

Some of the time they were able to talk together as they worked, and Don Vicente would speak of his experiences on the highways of Peru.

"If you think this is a difficult situation, I can tell you of the time when we drove up to the Apurímac Bridge only to find it was gone. Two trucks had fallen into the river and had been swept away with their drivers. It was only by good fortune that my *chulillo* called to me to stop in time. Then we waited in rain and gloom for six days before the soldiers came to put up a temporary bridge that would hold us."

"Ay, Don Vicente," said Carlos, shuddering at the idea, "how could the *Cóndor* cross on such a weak bridge?"

"I don't know how," answered the *piloto*, "but we all prayed to our favorite saints before we moved. Of course, I had all the passengers get off, and with their baggage, too. When I drove the *Cóndor* over, I was alone, and the bus was as light as a feather."

Carlos breathed a sigh. "I hope we never have such a problem."

"So do I," said Don Vicente with a grin.

And they went on with their work.

Another time, Don Vicente told Carlos about his brother, Edmundo, and how much he had been admired and respected by the other drivers.

"They told me how strict and fair he always was," said

Don Vicente. "He demanded that the work be done honestly and carefully. No one could touch the cargo except those who had checked it on board. And when he drove, no matter what kind of road it was, he was careful. Ay, there was a man who drove with his hands and his head, and with his heart, too."

So the hours passed, and the work went on.

Then, shortly before twilight, they heard the deep, growling sound of hard-working engines. They all put down their tools and buckets and listened. One of the children ran to the top of the mound of earth across the road and turned to them with a shout.

"The army! The army is here!"

All of them, masters and boys and passengers, ran up the hill to see. The *campesinos* stopped their work and they all watched two bulldozers come laboring toward them.

On the other side of the roadblock they saw four army trucks parked. Two were flatbeds and had held the tractors. The others were troop carriers, and about twenty soldiers were busy unloading their tools. Some were putting up tents in a small clear space beyond the road, and others were working their way down to the river with lines and poles to make a hoist for their water buckets.

As the people stood at the top of the landslide, they saw two officers walking toward them, followed by the noisy tractors. The people stood back from the drivers, and the soldiers came forward to greet them and talk over the situation.

"We came as soon as we had the news," said the older officer. "I hope we can have you moving soon."

"Our thanks, Captain," replied Don Vicente. "We have been here three days now, and we would not like to return to Cuzco."

"Of course not," said the captain. He turned to the drivers of the bulldozers.

"Ramón! Luis!"

"Yes, sir!" said the men as they came quickly.

"I think you must begin here at the summit, and then work downward. The men below will clear away what you push down. I believe we still have about two hours of working time before it is too dark."

"Yes, sir!" answered the soldiers.

Then, turning to the drivers, he said, "Be sure your people keep clear of this work now. I wish the *campesinos* to help us and work alongside the men in our unit."

"That's the kind of army I prefer," said Don Vicente as he walked back with Carlos. "There's plenty for them to fight against right here in our own country. It helps us all, and what's even better, no one is killed."

That night, after the work was over, most of the men and boys walked over the roadblock and visited the soldiers' camp. They sat beside the tents and talked with the soldiers, asking for news about road conditions. Gradually the talk lightened, and a soldier with his guitar sang some of the songs they knew.

Carlos stayed close to Don Vicente, who merely stood and listened after he had learned that the road was in good condition all the way to the coast. As the music grew louder, the men talked about the news of Lima, of jobs to be had there, and of the latest *fútbol* game in the stadium. The gathering grew noisier, and soon there were a few arguments springing up among the soldiers and the others. Voices were raised, and the music grew even louder. Then, suddenly, the officers signaled to their men.

Quickly the fires were banked, and the visitors were told that the camp was now to be closed. The soldiers began to settle themselves in their camp for the night while the men and boys returned over the roadblock to their buses and trucks.

Don Vicente nodded at Carlos and sent him to his

place at the rear of the bus. There was nothing to be said. They had done their work on the bus. It was clean and ready for the road, and the engine had been carefully checked. Tomorrow at this time, God willing, they would again be on their way toward Lima.

7

BEFORE IT WAS DAYLIGHT, CARLOS FELT A PERSISTENT shaking of his shoulder. He didn't want to open his eyes yet, but he heard the rough voice of Don Vicente.

"Come on, boy, it's time we got to our work. Get up now!"

"Yes, *maestro*," mumbled Carlos, stretching and looking out at the dull, dark sky.

On all sides, they heard the sounds of people stirring, mothers calling softly to their children, some gathering together their belongings, once more getting ready for the trip ahead of them.

While Don Vicente called together his passengers and ordered them to stay near the bus, Carlos carefully wiped off the windshields and paid special attention to the broad sign above that read EL CÓNDOR DORADO. He climbed onto the roof to straighten the cargo nets and place the baggage properly for traveling.

They could hear engines laboring to turn over after such a long time of idleness. Others coughed and spat, and, just as the hearts of the passengers sank, they would start with a roar. The air was filled now with the fumes of gasoline and exhaust, while the drivers tested their engines. It would not do for the roadblock to be cleared and then to hold up the entire line of vehicles with a sluggish engine.

Don Vicente had reached in under the hood and wiped off the dust and grime in some places and the excess moisture in others. Then, looking about at some of the other trucks and buses, he went to help with those that were still having trouble starting.

In the meantime, the bulldozers and soldiers had been working on the roadblock, and, with the help of the *campesinos,* they would soon be finished. None of the *chulillos* had time to get together, although Carlos did see Pablo wave at him from the distance. He could only wave in return and go on with his work.

Finally, with their engines roaring mightily and their tracks clanking, the bulldozers cleared away the last of the earth from the road. The officers walked among the trucks and buses, and designated the order of passage. No one would be trying to take first place, but all wanted the right to leave promptly, and the task of the army was to help avoid accidents and arguments on the road.

The drivers and their helpers knew there would be much dust ahead of them and that unless they spread out and left some distance between each vehicle, the rest of the trip could be quite dangerous. They would have to contend with poor visibility. Other vehicles on the other side of the roadblock would need their turn to pass as they headed into the mountains coming from the coast. Finally, trucks traveling too close together were very noisy, and the drivers would not hear oncoming vehicles or their horns if they were sounded.

Just before the procession began, the drivers and some of the passengers contributed some *soles* to the *campesinos* who had come to help. No one insisted on this, and the farmers did not expect it, but Carlos knew how useful even a few *soles* could be for these men who were so much like his own family.

As the engines were idling, and all the passengers were in their places, Pablo ran over to see Carlos.

"*Adiós,* Carlito!" he called. "Will you look for me in Lima?"

"Yes, of course," replied Carlos, "but where?"

"Come in the afternoons to the Plaza San Martín. I am often there. Have a happy voyage, Carlito!"

With that, he waved again and ran off on his thin legs to his master who was already impatient.

The soldiers signaled to each bus and truck in turn, and the drivers carefully maneuvered their way onto the clear road and drove off.

Don Vicente, too, took his turn and, with a wave and a nod to the officers, he gunned his engine. Once again they felt the hard, rough earth under them and saw the line of cars, trucks, and buses that waited on the other side of the roadblock.

Carlos, in his place on the roof of the *Cóndor,* could again feel the wind as it whistled through his *chullo.* In the far distance ahead of them he saw the road winding its way upward and then downward, with the small dust clouds following the trucks that had gone ahead.

And so they drove on, through the mountains past the Indian villages and the occasional towns. They rolled by terraced farmlands cut into the mountains, and sometimes they had to stop for a flock of sheep or a herd of llamas to cross the road. Carlos felt a pang of homesickness each time he saw the animals he had so often tended.

It rained for two days as they moved toward the coast through the lower ranges of the Andes, and Don Vicente drove the *Cóndor* as if it were full of eggs. He slowed almost to a stop to pass through torrents that flowed over the road, using the power of the engine to keep them from sinking into mud.

When it rained, Carlos was even more important to them, and he had to stay on the roof to keep watch. As he huddled there, Don Vicente had thrown him a heavy piece of canvas for a cover, but it was hardly enough to keep him dry and, in a short time he felt as wet as a drowned lamb. Still, he peered forward as well as he could, looking out for other vehicles and leaning downward from time to time to wipe off the windshield where the wiper arms did not reach.

Tired, weak, and dizzy, Carlos could hardly keep his grip on the net, when after several hours, the driver pulled to a stop in a small town near Puquio.

"Come down now, *hombre!*" he called to Carlos.

As the passengers got off the bus to have a hot meal in a small tavern sheltered from the rain, Don Vicente took Carlos' arm and led him in with them.

Don Vicente, who was well pleased with his *chulillo,* sat down beside him and ordered a meal for them both.

"Let's warm up with a good *caldo* and a fine *churrasco,*" he ordered.

Carlos was happy expecting the hot soup and the beefsteak, especially as he had never had such meat before. He waited patiently beside his master, feeling the warmth of the room, and hearing the talk of the other passengers who were seated at tables nearby.

For Carlos, the meal itself was a special part of his adventures, and he ate it quickly and gratefully. Don Vicente watched him with sidelong glances, noting how he relished the unfamiliar food and how quietly he sat when he was finished.

An unusual one, thought the driver, not quite like Edmundo, but a hard worker and a man just the same.

The rains stopped and the bus went on through the towns and villages, passing between the peaks of the mountains, and then they were at Nazca.

They had come gradually through lower and lower levels of the Andes, and Carlos watched for the wider expanses of farm and grazing land. Here, he could see, were farmers who could get more from the land. He saw the streams which were once rivers higher up in the mountains and which now only trickled down toward the ocean which Don Vicente said was only a few dozen miles away.

The road was better, with fewer sharp curves and a firmer surface, and at Nazca they saw a good-sized town and the famous Pan-American Highway. Now Carlos was amazed at the great numbers of new, fast automobiles that sped by. He could hardly count the trucks and buses which ran north to Lima and south toward Arequipa and the border with Chile.

Don Vicente reminded him of the desert war of the 1880's which he had learned about at school in Urubamba. The driver spoke bitterly of the Chileans and of how at last Peru was again master of the beautiful city of Tacna just at the border.

Then he added thoughtfully, "But we must not think too much about that. We have learned to live with our neighbors, and they also have their troubles."

As they drove north toward Lima, Carlos no longer rode above with the cargo, or on the ladder at the rear of the *Cóndor*. The road was wide; its surface was hard and well paved, and the visibility was good. He sat beside the driver and watched the traffic streaming in both directions. Behind them the passengers chatted restlessly, sensing that their long journey would soon be over.

Passing by crossroads, Carlos saw stands piled with fruits and vegetables that were unknown to him. These *mercaditos* at the sides of the road offered food to the many travelers on the *Carretera Panamericana*. Carlos almost wished they might stop so that he could see what there was, but he, too, found himself urging the *Cóndor* onward to Lima.

They stopped at Nazca, and after that came Ica, and at last, Pisco. Then, there was the ocean. Carlos had been straining his eyes for many miles, until Don Vicente nudged him.

"There," he said, "there is our great ocean. You can see it, and I am sure you can smell it, too."

"Yes," said Carlos, looking toward a mass of grey fog. He could not see any water, but there was a strong mixture of many strange smells he could not name. The smells floated all over the bus and brought him a sensation of the nearness of the sea, his mind picturing ships and fishermen, and the great waves of the seacoast. But of the ocean, Carlos saw nothing because of the fog.

Now the traffic became heavier and more congested. There were more cars and trucks and buses than ever. People were riding bicycles and on burros. Some drove little three-wheeled wagons, sitting behind them as if they were tricycles. Families walked along the road, and once Carlos saw a priest standing beside the road with a box in his hand, hoping that drivers would stop and give alms.

"Watch carefully," said Don Vicente, as he kept the *Cóndor* in the center lane of the highway. "We are so close to Lima now you can reach out and touch it. And the drivers are not all fine *pilotos,* so we will have to be very careful. I don't want to put any scratches on our *Cóndor* after so many long miles."

Carlos couldn't tell where to look first. The road was now like a river of traffic. There were buildings and houses on all sides. Some looked like factories, others were behind adobe walls and reminded him of the *barrios* in Cuzco where so many people lived.

He saw children playing alongside the road, some with

toys and dolls, others with stones and bits of wood. He almost saw his sister Martita again when they drove past a large building that had a Peruvian national shield over its door. A school, Don Vicente told him.

They were in the city, the great city of the Kings of Spain. Lima surrounded them—with buildings, with people, with its sounds and smells.

On some corners, Carlos saw the *anticuchos* cooking over outdoor broilers, the hot pungent aroma of the meat drifting toward the street. But the smell of gasoline was even stronger, and at first this was the smell of Lima for him.

As the *Cóndor* stopped at a sign from a policeman wearing white sleeves and white gloves, Carlos saw tall buildings reaching to the sky like some of his mountains at home. All kinds of automobiles drove alongside them, some with women at the wheel, others with drivers who called, *"Taxi!"* or *"Colectivo!"* waving their hands at the people on the sidewalk.

Ahead of them he saw what looked like a large wooden house rolling on tracks, swaying from side to side, and rumbling louder than mountain thunder. This was the streetcar he had heard about. As it went, Carlos saw the boys and young men who clustered about the back like flies, and who dropped off so skillfully that they never stumbled.

Carlos had many questions to ask his master, but he did not dare. Don Vicente gave his full attention to the problems of driving. He muttered and mumbled to himself as he gestured at drivers who came too close, or who refused to yield at an intersection. He swung the *Cóndor* around corners and around parked trucks and nodded with thanks at a policeman who waved him onward once when they faced a red traffic light.

Then, at last, Don Vicente nudged him again as he

pulled the *Cóndor Dorado* to the curb. With a sigh and a stretch, he opened the door and said, "Get busy, *chulillo,* we're in Lima now."

8

IT HAD TAKEN ONLY A SHORT TIME FOR CARLOS TO UNLOAD the baggage from the top of the *Cóndor*. The travelers were eager to take their belongings and go on their way in the great city. Some thanked him and pressed a few coins into his hand as they left. Others merely gathered their parcels, looked carefully onto slips of paper, and walked off.

Now that the *Cóndor* was unloaded, Carlos was not sure what he should do, but Don Vicente did not let him wait long.

"Let's get busy and get this bus good and clean," he ordered.

Carlos swept and washed the bus inside and out, while the driver worked over the engine. Anxious as he was to leave and find Ricardo, Carlos put the final touches on the sign that read EL CÓNDOR DORADO. Then he waited for Don Vicente.

Don Vicente walked all around the *Cóndor*, hands in his pockets, surveying what Carlos had done. He nodded only slightly, but his appreciation was clear.

"You have done well, *chico*," he said, "and now, let us arrange our account."

Carlos stood before his master, his sack at his feet, his *chullo* in his hand.

"I will give you ten *soles* for your work. As a beginner

you have done well enough, but with experience you will do even better. Have you any other money?"

Carlos nodded, "Yes, sir."

"I know," continued Don Vicente, "that you are not going with me on my next trip. My regular helper will be here tomorrow and he will have his job as before. But should you want me, you can always find me here when I am in Lima, at the Parque Universitario. Or you can ask for me at this café where they will know my schedules."

Carlos nodded again.

"Now remember," added the driver, "if you are ever in trouble, or if there is a serious matter, remember you are the brother of Edmundo Bernal, and you have been my *chulillo*. There are many here in the *parque* who will be ready to listen if there is need."

"Thank you, sir," said Carlos softly.

Don Vicente was silent for a moment, looking him over. This boy seemed so young to be going off alone. He had been a fine helper, but surely he would find Lima a hard, tough place to make his way. Still, many like him were streaming into Lima every day, and he would have to find his own road.

"Remember," he said gruffly, "keep that *chullo* out of sight. No one needs to know you're a *campesino*, even if you can read and write. Now, let's have a look at the address of your Ricardo Chambi."

Carlos handed him the slip of paper he had had in his sack and he listened carefully to the directions Don Vicente gave him. He was told where to find the right bus, what to give the driver, and what street to ask for. He must listen carefully to what was said, and to think before replying. Soon he would be with his friends, and they would help him make his plans.

"*Adiós, maestro,*" said Carlos, picking up his sack and holding a coin in his hand.

"*Adiós, adiós!*" answered the driver, "go, and may good fortune be with you. *Adiós.*"

Don Vicente turned away from Carlos and walked briskly into the café.

Now, in the midst of hurrying crowds, of noisy traffic, and tall buildings, Carlos felt very much alone. He walked away from the *Cóndor* which had been his care for such a long time. Lima was all around him and he must find his way.

As he had been told, he boarded the tired, dirty bus, and handed his money to the driver. Pressed among the crowded passengers, he swayed with them at each corner, and felt himself pushed and tugged each time someone wanted to get off. No one paid any attention to him, and he hoped the driver would remember to let him off at the street he had asked for.

Meanwhile, as well as he could, Carlos clutched his sack and tried to peer out the windows of the bus at the streets and avenues. He could see the tall buildings, the shops, the many carts being pushed or peddled like bicycles. People were everywhere, more people than he had ever seen together.

At last, the bus stopped and he heard the driver calling, *"Chico,* here you are!"

He saw the man's eyes fastened on him in the large rearview mirror, and then the door of the bus swung open and he felt himself nudged toward it.

He stepped down to the street as the bus started up behind him and roared away, spewing clouds of blue haze as it went. His heart beat faster, and he looked again and again at the slip of paper with Ricardo's address.

Beginning to walk down the street, he saw that there were no shops here. The houses were large, some of two stories, behind high brick or adobe walls. In each wall was a gate of metal or wood, and on top of some of the walls he could make out rolls of sharply barbed wire and pointed pieces of broken glass. As he passed, he could hear the barking of dogs behind some of the gates.

Comparing the address on the paper with the numbers on the gates, Carlos knew he was very near, and then, at last, here it was.

He stood in front of a wooden gate set into a brick wall. Now he was almost afraid to push the button. What if the address was wrong? What if Sarita and Ricardo were no longer here? A thousand doubts went through his mind at this moment, and he stood hesitantly.

Then, taking a deep breath, Carlos pressed the button and heard the bell ring far back in the house. For a time there were no other sounds, and then he heard footsteps.

The gate swung open slightly and a head looked around it at him.

"*Ay, hombre!*" shouted Ricardo. "It's you!"

Carlos smiled weakly. How he had looked forward to this moment! Ricardo grasped his arm and pulled him inside, clutching and embracing him and his sack at the same time.

Ricardo did not shout again, but his voice was warm and friendly. Here was his old friend from home. They had come together at last.

Carlos felt himself pulled along toward the side of the house. He could see it was a large two-story house, decorated with stones of different shapes and colors. There were colored tiles on the walls, and it was separated from the street wall by a well-planted garden.

Carrying his sack, Ricardo hurried Carlos into the house by a side door, and they went through a side yard toward the rear. There, he saw some large washtubs, crates standing about, and a small building attached to the main house. They entered one of the doors of this building and Ricardo put down the sack on the floor.

"This is my room," he announced. "Quite a difference from Urubamba, isn't is?"

Carlos agreed. It was almost as large as his family's whole house. It had an iron bed with a mattress and cover, a small table, and a tall wardrobe. A single electric light swung over their heads, and to one side a folded cot lay on the floor.

Carlos sat on the bed beside his friend, and they looked at one another.

He saw his schoolfriend was no longer a *campesino*. His eyes were bright and shining, but his hair was cut short and close to his head. He wore brown pants and sandals and a white shirt open at the neck.

Ricardo tried not to smile, looking at Carlos. Here,

indeed, was a *campesino,* with his short trousers coming just below the knee, an old dark shirt, and a felt hat. Surely his *chullo* must be there in the sack with his *poncho!*

Ricardo had many questions to ask. He wanted to know about his family and his other friends in Urubamba.

"And how is the *maestro,* Señor Valdez? What have you been doing, Carlito? Tell me! Tell me!"

Carlos answered as well as he could. He told about his friend's family. He explained about Edmundo's return to their home, and he described the plans they had been making to improve the school.

"We planned a petition, and we gathered signatures, even thumbprints. Padre Manya and Señor Valdez helped, and Edmundo had all the young men of the town talking to the parents. I think we can get one more teacher and have a larger school."

Ricardo sat on the edge of the bed and listened now, shaking his head in admiration. The people of Urubamba were his own, after all, and he felt pride in their efforts.

Then Carlos thought of something.

"But where is your sister?" he asked. "Does Sarita live here, too?"

"Of course," smiled Ricardo, "her room is next door with another girl. They're working in the house now. Sarita helps with the shopping, with the cooking, and with the cleaning."

"And you, Ricardo," asked Carlos, "what is your work here?"

"Ah," answered his friend, "I do many things. I work with the gardener and help to keep the grounds clean. Some days I help polish the floor and the furniture. The Master takes me with him to run errands in the city sometimes, and sometimes I go all by myself. The Señora lets me help to wait on table, and then I help to wash up in the kitchen afterwards. Oh, there are many things for me to do here."

Carlos could see that Ricardo was truly busy in this house. And yet, he seemed to have time, as now, for talking and resting in his room.

"Do you have time for yourself?" he asked. "What about our old ball games, and do you go to school also?"

"Ay, Carlito," answered Ricardo with a smile, "of course I have time to do things for myself. When the Señor and the Señora are not at home, we can get many things done quickly. And naturally, some of my errands take me a long way from here, so I can visit the city as I please."

Then he looked at Carlos for a moment, saying nothing.

"After all," he went on, "when you work for someone, you must be ready when they want you. There are schools in Lima, and not far from here. But I would never have the time to go to school now. My work keeps me too busy."

The two boys talked some more about how Ricardo's life had turned out in Lima and how lucky he was to have a fine job like this, with a comfortable room. Very few boys who came from the mountains could get such a pleasant job, with these comforts. And the labor was not like farm work, either.

Carlos told about his trip as a *chulillo* with Don Vicente, and he described all that had happened on the way. Now, he wanted to know, was there a job for him here with Ricardo? He was not going back to Urubamba, and Lima could become his home as it was now for Sarita and Ricardo.

Ricardo said, "Let me see what we can do. In the meantime, I must have the Señora's permission for you to stay with us. There is a place for you in my room, if she will allow you to remain. Remember, if she asks you, you are my cousin!"

Ricardo left him to stretch out on the bed while he went to see if the Señora would speak with him. As Ricardo went out, Carlos felt very strange in this room. He heard the noises of work in the house, of pans clattering in the kitchen, and of voices. From the distance, he could hear street noises, the barking of a dog, the horns of cars, and the high buzzing of an airplane.

He hoped that he might work here with Ricardo. It seemed just as if they were still the same old friends, and this would be a fine way to know Lima together. Well, the Señora must be kind and generous to provide such clothing and a room for a simple worker in her house.

Ricardo returned in a short time and with Sarita, his sister. She, too, greeted Carlos warmly and with kindness. She asked him many of the same questions that Ricardo had asked, and Carlos tried to answer them patiently and with courtesy. Sarita had become plumper than when she was in Urubamba, but her speech was more rapid and she was not the shy, reserved person he remembered.

Carlos looked at Ricardo, after a while, with questioning eyes. What had the Señora said? Would he be welcome here?

Ricardo knew what he was asking, but he did not look too happy.

"Understand, Carlito," he began, "there are many things to be done and enough people in the house to do them. So the Señora says she will allow you to stay with us for three days because you are our cousin. In the meantime, she will ask among her friends if there is a family who needs a helper."

Carlos was disappointed, but he could do nothing else. At least he would be glad to stay with his friends for a few days. Then he would go out and look for himself. Maybe he could even find his friend Pablo, the *chulillo*. "Remember," he had said to Carlos, "I am often in the Plaza San Martín in the afternoons."

The rest of that day and the next went by quickly.

Carlos slept on the little cot in Ricardo's room. He ate outside the kitchen door and did what he could to help the others in the house with their cleaning. But he was very shy and did not want to spend much time inside the house where the Señor and the Señora lived with their children.

The other servants paid him little attention, and being very busy most of the time, they rested during the spare moments they had. There were a gardener and a cook as well as a nurse for the children, and two servants, Sarita and Ricardo, who helped all the others.

Still, when there errands for Ricardo to the center of Lima, Carlos went also. They rode together once on the bus, and when they got off Ricardo showed him the heart of the city. They walked right beside the high buildings and peered at the posters outside the lavish movie houses. There were shops such as Carlos had never seen, some for clothing only, others for food, others with jewelry and trinkets. And he thought of Señor Rivera's shop in Urubamba, which had once seemed so grand!

They walked until Carlos complained that his feet were tired. The pavements were hot and hard, not like the cool fields of Urubamba. They rested in some of the small, green parks that were in many parts of Lima, even near the great Palace of the President. Sitting at ease, they watched the palace guards standing at their posts in brilliant plumed helmets and uniforms, swords glistening over shining spurs.

Later they passed over the Rímac River bridge to look at the oldest part of Lima. It was even more crowded than the other parts of the city Ricardo showed him, and the houses were quite old. Here, even the cars and buses were older and shabbier than elsewhere, and their noise and fumes made him gasp.

Ricardo felt himself quite the master of this great city, and he delighted in explaining it all to Carlos. He pointed out the important buildings and showed him the fine, broad avenues. He wanted Carlos to know Lima as he himself had learned to know and love it. No one would want to return to a place like Urubamba after coming to Lima.

The few days passed quickly. Carlos went with Ricardo on some of his errands, and he grew somewhat more familiar with the city. He was afraid to ask for news about a job, but he looked sadly at Sarita whenever she came to Ricardo's room. The time allowed by the Señora was soon over, and there was no word of a job for him. He would have to leave his friends and this house. What would he do now? With no work and no place to stay, Carlos could think only of the *parque* where he might find Don Vicente or some of the other *pilotos* who knew Edmundo. If he were a *chulillo* again, he could travel and work and still come to Lima some of the time.

Then he remembered his friend Pablo, who had been so cheerful when they worked together to clear the landslide. What was it Pablo had said?

"You can find me in the Plaza San Martín almost any afternoon!"

That afternoon Carlos and Ricardo set out for the plaza where he hoped to find Pablo. He had his sack with him, and he did not expect to return with Ricardo this time. After all, the Señora had made it clear that he could not stay on forever.

The plaza was beautiful today. The monument to the great General San Martín was decorated with flowers and wreaths. He sat on his horse, facing the Hotel Bolívar as if to greet the tourists who came and went there each day.

Carlos loved the Plaza San Martín because it was lined with shops that had beautiful things for sale. On one side of the plaza were the movie houses where he loved to stand and look at the posters telling about the pictures which he had never seen. Ricardo had told him how wonderful they were, but he could not use his money yet, not for pictures, when he didn't know where he would live or work.

Walking into the plaza, the boys saw many people

strolling and sitting on the cool, shaded benches. There were boys selling newspapers, calling out the latest headlines. Other boys were offering lottery tickets to each passerby, promising a sure winner in next Sunday's drawing. Then there were the shoeshine boys, each carrying his box ready to drop to the ground and go to work at anyone's nod.

Ricardo reminded Carlos that he could not stay too long.

"You know," he said, "the Señor has sent me on an errand and even such an errand cannot keep me away too long."

"I understand," answered Carlos, as they walked about almost aimlessly, looking among all the different boys who came and went in plaza.

The hour grew later and still there was no sign of Pablo. At last, Ricardo said he would have to go.

"But remember," he said, "if you have no place to stay tonight, be at our gate around eleven o'clock. I will be near the gate to let you in, so be sure not to ring. The Señora will never know that you stayed with us. But don't worry, you'll find your friend soon, anyway."

Carlos felt helpless and defeated. He still had no job and not even a place to stay, unless his friend Ricardo lied to his employers and hid him. Well, maybe it was for the best. He had seen wonderful Lima, and now it was time to go home.

"*Adiós,* Carlito," said Ricardo, gripping his arm. "I know you will find your way. And when I need you I will come to the plaza in the afternoon. The Señora told me she would be looking for a job for you."

"Ay, Ricardo, I hope you will come and find me soon. I would hate to return to Urubamba now."

"*Adiós, hombre,*" whispered Ricardo, and he ran off toward the busy streets on his errands.

Carlos wandered about now, feeling lost, but still in

awe of all the activity he saw going on at every side. The plaza was a busy place, with boys and men going about their business, or just sitting lazily, watching the others.

After a while, he noticed some boys on the grass who were kicking a ball about. The ball was passed from one to the other just as in the *fútbol* matches he used to play on the field near the school in Urubamba. The boys shouted to one another, called jeers at a bad play, and seemed to be happy in their game on the cool grass.

Then, as he walked over closer to watch the game, one of the boys turned his head toward him and he recognized his friend Pablo. What luck!

"Pablo!" he called. "Hey, Pablo!"

The boy walked out of the game, still watching the ball, and then he turned toward the young *campesino* who had called. With a shout, he grabbed Carlos' arms and whirled him around.

"Hombre!" he yelled, "it's you! I'm glad to see you! How long are you in Lima?"

Carlos could hardly catch his breath, but he walked along with Pablo, happy to be with a friend again.

They both began to talk at once, but finally Pablo listened while Carlos told about his trip to Lima and how he had stayed with his friends.

"And now," said Pablo, "you have no place to stay and no job?"

Carlos nodded.

"Well," said Pablo, picking up his shoeshine box and leading Carlos to a bench where they could sit down, "one thing we don't need is another one with a box like this. Why don't you find Don Vicente and just go back home?"

Carlos looked at him, hardly able to speak. He wanted to stand up and go on his way. This Pablo was not his friend.

"No," said Pablo with a wry smile. "You're not going back to your town and your family and that little piece of

land. Not yet. Not until you've seen all of Lima. Not until you've learned to hate it a little, the way many *campesinos* do when they can no longer go back to the *altiplano*. Don't you know some people hate Lima because it is hard and treacherous? They say they lose their families here and no one cares."

Carlos looked at Pablo, somewhat surprised. He had never heard talk like this, and yet he thought Pablo had never been so serious before.

"Yes," said Pablo, "there are too many in Lima now, and more are always coming. It is a place of beauty, but also of much sadness."

Pablo caught Carlos' worried expression, and he quickly brightened his own.

"What am I saying?" he said. "You've just arrived and I'm already telling you terrible things! Never mind. We'll find work for you, and in the meantime, you're coming home with me!"

He waved a farewell to his friends in the ball game and some of them waved back. Shouldering his shoeshine box on its strap, Pablo led Carlos out of the plaza, once more toward the Rímac River where the Spanish had first settled.

9

CARLOS LAY ON HIS BACK BESIDE PABLO, WHO WAS ALREADY curled up and sleeping. The shack was small, made of old boards, adobe blocks, and whatever the family had found to make a shelter. He could not sleep, but he remembered the afternoon and evening when he met Pablo's family and they had welcomed him warmly. No señora here had told him he could stay only three days.

The sounds of music and laughter drifted toward him as he lay in his poncho on a mound of hard straw and old newspapers. They had eaten their meal of rice, with bits of *ají,* the strong pepper they all loved. Then, by the light of some candles, the brothers and sisters of Pablo had begun to ask him about his family and his trip to Lima.

Pablo's mother was friendly, a warm, round woman who seemed not to mind another guest who became a member of the family without notice. He could share their rice, and one day he would add his *sol* to the family market money. They had talked for what seemed to Carlos like many hours. Neighbors from other shacks in the *barriada* had stopped in, and all were friendly, but they were also very poor.

Pablo had led Carlos across the Rímac River bridge and along the streets of the old town until they found a dirty, almost broken-down bus. This, said Pablo, would take them to Fray Martin de Porres, the *barriada* where his family lived. Carlos parted with a few *centavos* for them both, since he was not in the mood for hanging dangerously onto the rear of the bus. Besides, Pablo warned him, this driver knew that most of his passengers would rather ride without paying, and he watched zealously for any who might be hanging on under the cracked rear window.

At last they found themselves in a city like none Carlos had seen before, in the *altiplano,* on the highway, or even in Lima. The streets were lined with little shacks made of almost any kind of boards, stones, bits of posters, and highway signs. Children played in the muddy streets, dabbling their hands in the water, and without care for the bus or the little wagons which went by.

At some corners there were water faucets from which the women took their water for cooking, washing, or drinking. There were no street lights, but some shops had been set up for the people of the *barriada,* and the kerosine lamps cast their brightness onto the street. Here, Pablo told him, no one paid rent, for they had "invaded" the unused land and taken it from the city because there was no other place to go. Often the police came and tried to remove people, but there were too many now, and the police could not put their hearts into the task.

"So you see," Pablo told him, "we have a place to live where we can be together. Many of the men work in other parts of Lima and go each day to Miraflores or to San Isidro to earn some *soles*. My brothers and I go, also, but so far we have only shoes to shine and newspapers to sell."

Carlos was thinking of the fine room in the great house where Sarita and Ricardo had welcomed him. This *barriada* reminded him of places in Cuzco where he had been. Even in Urubamba the smells had not been so bad or the streets so dirty! But above all, Carlos felt weary and unhappy. Lima was turning out to be so many different things all at once.

In the days that followed, Carlos spent much time with Pablo and his brothers. They roamed the city, finding shoes to shine, newspapers to sell. Pablo even sold some lottery tickets for a while, until some older boys drove him from a good corner in one of the smaller plazas.

Carlos learned to place his shoeshine box down smartly in front of a man who looked like a customer, so quickly that the man could hardly say no. He learned to watch out for the police, judging which would look the other way as he worked and which would tell him to pick up his box and move on.

One place Carlos wanted to avoid was the Parque Universitario, where Don Vicente had said he could be found. He was still not ready to seek help, and Lima was now becoming friendlier.

He lived with Pablo and his family, sharing his few *soles* and the joys of the family. He knew when to be still and listen as their mother, Señora Maria, gave her orders to them all, and he knew when he could join in the talk about the day's work.

The boys went all over Lima, from the Rímac to the beach at La Herradura, carrying their shoeshine boxes. They stopped to look at shiny automobiles, at beautiful gardens, and they pressed their noses against lavish shop windows.

Carlos learned how to pass a fruit stand outside a *mercado* and snatch a banana or an apple, making off with it quickly through the crowd. He could be a *pájaro frutero* as well as any of the boys. But he also knew that the stolen fruit was not really his if a larger boy saw him and grabbed it from him.

Carlos had learned many things about how to live in

Lima. But he was still a quiet boy. He could not chatter away as Pablo did, or boast of his exploits in the *mercado* as the others did. He enjoyed their games of *fútbol* in the park and the times when they sat on the grass and shared their hopes for the next day or the next week.

Few of the boys had been as far in school as Carlos had, and when he told them in his soft words of the petition for the school in Urubamba, he could tell they didn't understand. Maybe it was because they didn't know anyone like his teacher, Señor Valdez, he thought. But after that, he didn't speak much of such things. Instead, he loved to tell about his brother Edmundo, who had been a famous *piloto*, and who had driven huge trucks over the highways of Peru. Then they listened, and some of the boys wished they might be like Edmundo someday. So did Carlos, in his own mind, but he knew how hard it was, even if Don Vicente had said he might be a *chulillo* again.

The days and weeks passed in this way, Carlos earning a few *soles* and contributing them to his adopted family where Dona Maria considered him as one of her own. She mended his trousers and his shirt, and washed what he had so that he could be clean, as she insisted they must all try to be in her family.

He now knew Lima well, having marveled at the huge ships in Callao harbor, and having watched the airplanes taking off and landing at the beautiful airport. He found his way easily to all the important plazas, and he could ride without fear on the outside of the streetcars as the others did.

Then, one day, as he followed Pablo and some of the other boys through the Plaza San Martín, just beside the statue he heard someone shouting his name.

"Carlito! Carlito!" he heard.

Turning quickly he saw Ricardo waving his hand, hurrying toward him.

"*Caray!*" he said panting, "I could hardly catch you! Wait for me now, won't you?"

Carlos was truly glad to see Ricardo, for he had had no news of him since they had said goodbye weeks ago. Ricardo would also have news of Urubamba, Carlos thought. He had not sent word home himself, since he had arrived, and he felt suddenly ashamed.

Now he greeted Ricardo warmly, delighted to see how well he looked.

"*Que tal, hombre?*" asked Carlos, feeling as if he were a fellow *Limeño*. "How are things with you?"

"*Bien,*" replied Ricardo, "*ay,* how I have searched for you this week. I've been here in the plaza every day, and the Señora has sent me herself!"

Carlos took a deep breath. He couldn't ask, but he saw a smile on Ricardo's face, and he waited.

"There is a job for you," said Ricardo, "with a family not far from our house. The Señora asked if they could use a helper, and they want to see you. It must be right away. They have waited several days already."

"Yes," answered Carlos thoughtfully, "I think I would like such a job. But I have been working and earning money, so maybe I shouldn't take a new job now."

"*Ay!*" shouted Ricardo, "don't be a fool! You cannot run around stealing and shining shoes and hope to make something of yourself. And you won't earn seventy-five *soles* a month with meals and clothing that way, either!"

Carlos could hardly believe what he had heard. This was a job for him, after all.

He presented Ricardo to Pablo and his other friends and told them that he might have a job. Some of them looked envious, and others seemed to think there was no job in Lima as good as theirs now. As for Pablo, he only said, "Let's go home. You can get your things. I guess my mother will be sorry to see you go."

Ricardo went with them to the *barriada,* and he greeted Doña Maria politely, explaining how he and Carlos had been friends in Urubamba.

The children all said a hasty goodbye to Carlos, but Pablo stood outside the door and hardly looked at him. Doña Maria gave Carlos a warm embrace and squeezed his head to her bosom for a moment. Then she patted him on the shoulder and pushed him toward the street. Carlos took his sack and went out with Ricardo. He hoped Pablo would be his usual grinning, active self, but he only stood there, with his face turned away.

Carlos said, "*Adiós,* Pablito, may you have good fortune."

But Pablo merely scratched in the dirt of the street with his torn shoe and refused to speak. Carlos put his hand out toward him, but he backed away and was silent. At last, Carlos put his sack over his shoulder and pushed Ricardo on, leaving Pablo's family, his little shack, and Pablo himself.

They had gone only a few yards when he felt himself being turned, and Pablo had clutched his arms. With a fierce look, the boy embraced his friend and said hoarsely, "Don't forget us! We'll be here if you need us. Don't forget!"

Carlos barely had time to say yes in return, when Pablo dropped his arms and ran swiftly back into the shack. He was gone, but Carlos would always remember.

10

Wearing a white coat, Carlos stood behind the counter of the drugstore and neatly wrapped a package for a customer. He smiled, said, *"Gracias, señor,"* and handed the parcel across the counter. As he did so, he glanced quickly toward Señora Fernandez, who presided over the cash register and whose family owned the store.

She was seated comfortably with a little magazine in front of her, but from time to time her eyes flew to all parts of the store. They checked and tested. They examined and counted everything. And, when they passed over to Carlos, he felt once again as he did the first day in the store, that he dared make no mistakes.

Although by now Carlos knew his simple tasks well, he was always careful. For the Señora could be angry, and she could make the world tremble before her. He had seen her scold the girl who worked at the other counter until she wept and begged for another chance. He, too, had felt her scorn when he had made some foolish mistake, and although weeping was not for men, Carlos had never known so harsh a taskmaster. At such times, he remembered Don Vicente as a kindly man, gentle and pleasant.

Now, when the Señora's eyes swept over him, he thought of the first days when Ricardo had brought him to the house of the Fernandez family. The master was away on business, but how the lady of the house had questioned him!

What was his name? Where were his parents? What had he been doing in Lima? And she was horrified and almost sent him away when he spoke of his days in the *barriada*. But, when Ricardo politely mentioned that Carlos could read and write Spanish well, she stopped and thought for a few moments.

"All right," the Señora had said, "you will have a place here, and you will work in the *farmacia*. Are you ready now?"

Carlos nodded and was truly afraid to ask about his wages, but Ricardo spoke again.

"Thank you, señora," he said, "and may we write to our family in Urubamba and tell them of his good fortune?"

He asked his question, pausing slightly at the end, and the Señora understood.

"Yes," she said gruffly, "tell them he will have his

• 105

meals, his clothes, his room, and seventy-five *soles*. Now, go to the *mayordomo* and he will show you your place!"

With that, she turned away and walked heavily to the door. Carlos smiled shyly as they went out to the back of the house, but she saw nothing. She only shouted for Hipólito to come and see the new boy.

The older man who was the chief servant of the Fernandez household led them to a small room very much like the room Ricardo had where he worked. After scolding the boys for being too noisy, Hipólito told Carlos to come later to the kitchen, and he left them alone.

Ricardo happily fell upon the bed and wrestled Carlos down beside him.

"You see," he laughed, "now you can be a real *Limeño*, instead of a thieving *pájaro* in the market. You will work and earn money, just as I do. And when we have a holiday, what fun we shall have together!"

Carlos was worried about the stern, severe Señora, but he looked about his room and thought how different it was. Here was no shack with old straw and bits of cardboard and cloth. He had an electric light over his head. There was water right outside his room and a kitchen nearby. Even in Urubamba, there was no house like this one which was now his!

"*Ay*, Ricardo," he said, "what good times we shall have together! We'll meet in the park, and we'll save our *soles* and go to the movies. We'll play *fútbol* and lie on the grass!"

"Yes!" shouted his friend, and then suddenly he stopped.

"How long I've been away! The master will behead me, and the Señora will scold until midnight. I must be gone. Do a good job, Carlito. I'll see you soon!"

With that, he dashed out of the room, stopping just long enough to pound his friend roughly on the shoulder.

And Carlos, alone, looked about him once more. He could hardly believe it. Of all the *campesinos* who came to Lima, he must be the only one to find so good a place. How the boys in the Plaza San Martín would envy him if they could see him! And this room, in this house!

He thought of Pablo and, for some reason, he no longer felt as happy. This was a fine room, but here was no Doña Maria, whose warmth and kindness had comforted him. Here was no crowd of noisy children to share his *soles* with and to play with in the *barriada*.

Then he heard Hipólito calling him, and the dark, stocky man who was in charge of the household was reminding him that there was food in the kitchen.

In the next days and weeks they became quiet friends, Carlos and Hipólito. Julia, the cook, who was Hipólito's wife, saw to it that he had enough to eat. She, too, was gruff, and seemed to be an imitation of the Señora. But when she noticed that his shirt was torn, she took it from him to mend without a word. The first few days after his arrival, Julia woke him softly in the morning to make sure he would be on time for work and not be scolded. After that, he would wake himself in time and they would eat together. Then he would be off for the drugstore on his bicycle. Julia and Hipólito had no children, and they both seemed to want to look after Carlos as long as he needed them.

As for his job, Carlos found it very exciting from the first. Even the ride to the city on the bicycle brought him joy. He rode along briskly, keeping a sharp eye for the cars and buses that were everywhere. He would go slowly by the stores with their beautiful displays, past the tall new buildings that were almost everywhere, and alongside the powerful blue buses that carried people into the heart of the city. And when he rode past one of the old churches, he would hold on with one hand and cross himself with the other. Some of the boys laughed at him as they rode together through the city, but Carlos remembered Padre Manya of Urubamba and the good manners he had been taught.

At the drugstore, there was no end of jobs to be done. He swept the sidewalk and the street in front of the store. He carried boxes from delivery trucks into the store. He made stacks of goods on the shelves and counted what there was. He helped the Señora when she came to the store later in the morning, and told her what was needed.

There was an older woman who came early also, and who helped Señora Fernandez, but she was a tall, silent person, who hardly spoke to Carlos at first, except to give him orders. Señorita Ysabel helped with prescriptions and gave injections, just as the Señora did. She had been to high school in Lima, and she came from an old family.

Carlos learned later that the Señora had also finished high school, and had even been to the university where she learned to be a pharmacist. That is what Señorita Ysabel had told him when they were better acquainted.

Carlos found his work easy to do although there were so many different tasks. Sometimes he was sent to other stores to get a special package, or to the home of a sick person to deliver medicine. These times were especially exciting for Carlos because then he could ride his bicycle and see more of Lima. Once he went on an errand and passed through the Plaza San Martín. He rode very slowly, hoping to catch sight of Pablo or some of the other *pájaros* with their shoeshine boxes and their strings of lottery tickets. There were boys in the plaza as always, but when Carlos stopped to ask about his friends, they eyed him coldly and told him nothing.

Another time, he thought, and he rode his bicycle off slowly. He had had no other chances to look for his friends. The *barriada* where Pablo and his family lived was too far away, and no drugstore ever sent medicines into that neighborhood. Most of his Sundays, Carlos spent with Ricardo, who didn't care to go visiting in the Fray Martin de Porres district.

With Ricardo, he went almost all over Lima. Their Sundays were spent happily. After church, where Carlos insisted on attending early mass, and where Ricardo reluctantly followed, they would go off to one of the parks and play soccer with other boys. Both he and Ricardo had orders from their Señoras to be home early in the afternoon, so it was not quite a fiesta every time. If they rode off in one of the huge streetcars to the harbor at Callao, they had to watch the time carefully. No boy with a good job wanted to risk losing it just for a bit of fun. So Carlos learned to be careful and to go and come on time wherever he was sent, even on Sundays.

Once, when he had taken a package to another drugstore, he stopped on the way to watch the soldiers at the President's Palace in the Plaza de Armas. He was fascinated by their colorful uniforms and their precise movements. The shouted commands made them turn and stamp and wheel in rigid formations. Carlos watched the changing of the guard in front of the imposing palace, and he reluctantly turned his bicycle back toward the store. The blare of the trumpets still sounded in his ears, and he narrowly missed running into a truck as he remembered the soldiers.

But when he returned to the store and put his bicycle away, he was met by the angry Señora.

"Miserable boy!" she shouted, "don't you care for your place here? You are paid to work, not to count all the loafers in Lima! When you are sent on an errand, you are expected back promptly, or you will suffer for it! . . ."

She had to take a deep breath before she could go on.

There was nothing Carlos could say. He had often stayed longer than an errand required, to see interesting things. Could he tell her how fascinated he had been by the soldiers at the President's Palace? There wasn't anything to

be said, just to listen and not anger the Señora any more. He did not want to lose his job. Where would he go then?

The Señora's anger diminished slowly, but not before she had warned him severely again, and not before she had told him what a stupid farmboy he was.

No one had ever spoken this way to Carlos, not even Don Vicente on the *Cóndor,* when the weather and road were miserable and Carlos had been slow in helping. Still, Carlos clenched his teeth and determined not to become angry as she was. It was not his way, and he waited for her wrath to subside.

For several days after that, Carlos did his errands almost with haste, to show the Señora that he knew what was expected of him.

As the days passed, Carlos came to know where all the packages were in the store. He knew how to stack them and where to put newly delivered merchandise. He also came to know Lima very well, having explored its narrow *jirónes* and its broad avenues with Ricardo and on work days when he could stretch out his errands without arousing the anger of Señora Fernandez.

Each week he counted over his little store of *soles* and he set aside one or two for a special treat when he and Ricardo were out together. They would buy savory, hot *anticuchos,* the rich meat on bamboo skewers. Or they would eat the spicy little *butifarras,* sandwiches of ham and cheese sold near the parks. There was always something tasty to be bought on the streets of Lima.

Once in a while, Carlos took a dozen or more of his *soles* to the post office, where Ricardo showed him how the money could be sent to his parents in Urubamba. He wrote some letters home, telling of his joys in Lima, of his good health, describing his work. He wished God to watch over and bless his parents, his brother and sister, and his grandmother.

Less often, letters came in the childish scrawl of Martita or in the strong, crude handwriting of Edmundo.

"My brother, Carlito," wrote Marta, "our father and mother send you their greetings. Also our *abuelita* sends hers. We work on the land. I go to school now, and Señor Valdez is my teacher. Edmundo is feeling well and works hard. He sends you greetings. We have had rain. May you keep well. Go with God."

Marta's letters almost brought back to Carlos her face and her voice, but he was not sure of them any longer. He could picture her as she was when he left their home months ago, but now he was not sure. He longed to talk again with his parents, to walk beside his father across the stony fields, to watch his mother at her work. When he closed his eyes, he could hardly bring back to mind their little house with its smoky air, the rustling of the chickens, and the sounds of the sheep outside.

He felt a sadness that he couldn't talk about with Ricardo or Sarita. Once, after he had received a letter, he sat quietly near Julia and Hipólito in the kitchen, watching them at their work. Only then did he feel a strange calm, and their soft voices soothed him with a sudden comfort.

When he had a letter from Edmundo, the news was more complete. The people had prepared their petitions for a school, but Padre Manya and Señor Valdez were not sure yet what they should do. No one felt safe in antagonizing Señor Rivera, the storekeeper, or Don Manuel, the owner of the *hacienda* where so many worked.

But both the padre and the teacher were encouraging the people. They would find that they had friends both in Cuzco and in Lima. And the school would surely be made into a six-year school! No, Edmundo himself was very hopeful, and his letter stirred a happy feeling in Carlos despite his homesickness.

Edmundo wrote also that his health was better and that he and their father were working the land together. Their parents thanked Carlos for the *soles;* mama had bought some new shoes and a *manta* last week. He must work hard at his job. He must learn all he could. He must try to improve himself and go to school. Were there no evening schools in Lima?

When he read this, Carlos was troubled. He had learned all there was to learn about his job. Señorita Ysabel and Señora Fernandez kept him busy enough, but his job was to lift and carry, to go and fetch and to return. He was a good sweeper of floors and of sidewalks, and he rode his bicycle carefully. This was his job, and while he found it easy enough, he needed no more schooling to do it better. He could go on with it as long as he was strong enough, and as long as he pleased Señora Fernandez.

He and Ricardo had often talked about going to school in the evening. There were such schools in Lima, and students were welcomed. But their Señoras would not hear of their leaving the house after the evening meal. Who could tell what mischief they might get into? Why did they need to learn so much anyway? They would only find bad company and thieves on the streets after dark.

No, evening school was for *Limeños* who lived with their families, or for *pájaros* who could come and go as they pleased. But Carlos had been a *pájaro,* and there were no *soles* each month for them, and no food each day, nor clothing given by the Señora.

Carlos thought of his days at school with Señor Valdez. He remembered the happy thoughts and hopes he and Ricardo had had as they dreamed together of Lima, where all kinds of splendors would lie at their feet.

His dreams had come true, but they were surrounded by poverty and hard work. They gleamed beyond the dirt of the *barriadas* and were tarnished by the sadness of people without homes. Carlos knew Lima well, now, and he loved this city, but how he wished he had Señor Valdez to talk with, and Padre Manya to help him ease his mind and reassure him.

He and Ricardo continued to be strong friends. They spoke frankly to each other and shared their plans. Ricardo wanted to save his money and go with his sister into some business where they could become rich. They would buy things at the market and go from door to door to sell. It did not matter what; Lima was a wonderful place for a young man to have his own business. In the meantime, he, too, with Sarita, sent a few *soles* home to their family in Urubamba.

Carlos wasn't sure. Sometimes he thought he would like to join his friends in their plans for business. Sometimes he thought with regret of Don Vicente and the *Cóndor*. How he had enjoyed the work on the bus! He could do what Edmundo had done. He could in time become a *piloto* and drive the huge trucks on the highways of the mountains and the coast. But once, when he visited Don Vicente in the Parque Universitario, he had mentioned his idea timidly. Don Vicente did not laugh, but he put his arm on Carlos' shoulder.

"*Hombre*," he said, "of course you could become a great *piloto*, but remember you are too young yet!"

"I could work as a *chulillo* again," offered Carlos.

"*Ay*," laughed Don Vicente, "for thirty *soles* a month and buy your own food and clothing? You do better than that now at your *farmacia!*"

Carlos had no other answer. And when he and Ricardo discussed their plans, he had very little enthusiasm.

He had been in Lima nearly a year. He worked as usual. He avoided the wrath of Señora Fernandez, and tried to be friendly with Señorita Ysabel. Julia and Hipólito were his friends at home, and he and Ricardo roamed through the city whenever they could.

Then, one day, as he returned from an errand he walked his bicycle across the avenue toward the *Farmacia* Fernandez. A truck was parked in front of the store, and, as Carlos reached the sidewalk, the driver opened his door and got out. Carlos saw the powerful-looking man in the leather jacket and dark trousers. Then he looked again and stopped.

"Edmundo!" he shouted. "It's you! It's you!"

He rushed to his brother and they embraced strongly, Edmundo pounding his back with vigor.

Then, there on the sidewalk in front of the drugstore, Edmundo held him at arm's length.

"Look at you," he said, "you are no longer Carlito, my little brother. You are almost a man! *Hombre,* it's good to see you!"

Carlos could hardly speak. He looked with pride at this strong, handsome young man. This was his brother, the famous *piloto,* who now had come to Lima for him.

"Come," said Edmundo, "I have much to tell you. Put away the bicycle and let's go."

Carlos suddenly realized that he had a job and that the wrath of the Señora would be kindled to an explosion if he said he must now take time off to go and talk with this brother of his. Edmundo noticed his hesitation and knew what must be done.

He watched Carlos put his bicycle in its rack. Then he

took him by the arm and walked with him into the store, right up to the Señora.

Tipping his driver's cap politely, he spoke with courtesy about himself.

"Kind lady," he said, "I am the brother of your employee, here, and I have just arrived from the mountains where our family lives. We have important matters to discuss before I make my next trip. Surely you can excuse him for the rest of the day to receive the blessing of his parents."

He spoke soothingly, and seemed to know the kind of person he faced.

Carlos watched as the wrinkles on the Señora's brow smoothed out and her cheeks and ears began to turn red. Ah, he thought, here comes the explosion!

But Edmundo saw this, too, and he added a few more words to convince her.

"*Ay*, señora," he said softly, "I have heard so much of your kindness from my *compañeros* who make deliveries to your *farmacia*. You know, we share our experiences and exchange our impressions of people. We talk about those we meet and, often, we can be of special help to them when we make deliveries."

This seemed to awaken the Señora at last. She had sudden visions of truck drivers making late deliveries to the *Farmacia* Fernandez. She imagined cases of goods carelessly handled, with broken bottles that would take weeks to replace. And she recalled the drivers to whom she sometimes gave chocolates, cigarettes, or other little gifts, for being very careful, and for giving special help with the stacking and placing of heavy packages. Edmundo and his *compañeros* were, indeed, important people. Certainly more important than a few hours of time of her delivery boy. Besides, she could send next door to borrow the grocer's boy and his bicycle in case of emergency.

With a wave of her hand, she gestured at the wide-eyed Carlos.

"Go then, and be with your brother," she said, "and be here on time in the morning."

And to Edmundo, she forced a reluctant smile. "I am glad your *compañeros* speak well of us. Remind them not to forget."

Almost weak with admiration, Carlos followed Edmundo out the door. They mounted to the cab of the truck, and Carlos watched as Edmundo maneuvered his way into the Lima traffic.

11

CARLOS WOULD REMEMBER THAT NIGHT ALL HIS LIFE. His brother had driven to a parking area near the Parque Universitario, where many trucks and buses were stationed. Leaving the truck safely, they had taken a taxi to Lince, another section of Lima, where Edmundo rang the bell at the front gate of a small, plain-looking house. An older woman opened the door and reached her hand out to Edmundo.

"Come in, come in," she said, smiling. "How are you, Edmundo? And is this Carlos?"

Carlos saw a slender, tall woman, with gray hair and a black dress. Her house was not nearly as well furnished as that of the Señora Fernandez. The furniture was plain and old, and the windows had curtains that kept out the light.

When Edmundo came into the house, he had removed his hat, and he smiled at the lady who greeted them.

"Yes, Doña Elvira, this is my young brother of whom I spoke."

She held her hand out to Carlos and then said, "Please sit down. Rosita will be here in a moment."

Edmundo smiled again and glanced quickly at Carlos. Then, hearing footsteps, he stood up and waited expectantly. Carlos stood also as a young woman came into the room and held out her hands to his brother. Edmundo led her toward Carlos and said, with pride in his voice, "Carlito, this is Rosa. We are to be married soon."

Carlos' heart jumped and he took the young woman's hand and shook it. He felt her warmth on his hand. She smiled at him and said, "I have heard so much about you, Carlos, and I am proud that we shall be relatives. I hope we will be well acquainted soon."

As Doña Elvira bustled about, preparing to serve coffee and cookies, Edmundo and Rosa sat down together and became engrossed in a private conversation. Carlos sat quietly and watched them. Rosa was tall for a girl, though not quite as tall as Edmundo. Her hair was black and came to her shoulders. Her eyes were a sparkling black and, when she smiled, he could see a little dimple in her cheek. She didn't look like a girl of the *altiplano,* but was much more Spanish, a true *Limeña.*

After a short time, Edmundo stood up and said they could not stay too long. They thanked Doña Elvira, and he shook hands with his fiancée before they left. Carlos murmured his thanks and followed Edmundo out.

This time in another taxi, Edmundo explained things to Carlos. He had met Rosa and her mother in Piura, in the far north of the country, on one of his first trips after leaving Urubamba. Rosa was a teacher in a country school and lived with her mother. They had met often and had written whenever he was not able to reach Piura. Rosa was a kind, gentle person, who admired Edmundo's strength and his good judgment.

"So you see, Carlos," said Edmundo, "now that I am in good health again, I am a *piloto* once more."

Carlos nodded his head, wide eyed.

"And," continued his brother, "Rosa and I will be married early in the coming spring, and we will live in Lima."

"Will you still drive on the great *carreteras,*" asked Carlos, "even when you are married?"

"Well," answered Edmundo, "Rosa will be a teacher here in Lima and Doña Elvira will live with us. She will keep Rosa company while I am away."

"Besides," he added thoughtfully, "I might work even harder for the transport company and become a dispatcher. Maybe I might someday be a manager. Then I would be in Lima all the time."

Carlos glanced at his brother. This was a new Edmundo. He no longer spoke fiercely and proudly of his adventures as a *piloto*. He dreamed instead of a house and a wife and family and, even more surprising, of becoming a dull *Limeño* for good. It almost shocked Carlos to think that a *piloto* would rather stay snug and warm in the office of the company as a dispatcher or a manager and send other men off to adventure and excitement.

Before he could say what he thought, their taxi stopped, this time in front of a small building that looked like a hotel. Again, Edmundo led the way and they entered the old adobe-and-wood structure, climbing a flight of stairs to a floor with a row of doors. Edmundo knocked, and Carlos heard a familiar voice call, "Enter!"

When they walked into the room, there was his friend and teacher, Señor Valdez. Forgetting his many thoughts, Carlos embraced his friend warmly, sensing only another homecoming. He could almost picture them together once more in Urubamba, rather than in a small, musty hotel room in Lima. Señor Valdez looked the same—dark, his curved Indian nose dominating his face, his straight lips smiling broadly, and his eyes wide and full.

"*Ay,* Carlos," said Señor Valdez, "what a pleasure it is to see you. Are you already a *Limeño?* Wait, let me see. . . . No, I think not yet. How strong you have grown, and taller!"

Carlos smiled at him and said, also, what a great pleasure it was to see his teacher again, and here in Lima. He no longer felt as shy as he did when in Urubamba and in school. After all, they were men together here, and good friends. But he could still not help his feeling of awe toward this man whom Carlos had first known when he was an ignorant child, and who had taught him so much.

Later in the evening, over a simple dinner at the hotel, the three men sat together and talked. Señor Valdez listened as Edmundo spoke with his brother.

"I told you, Carlito," he began, "that we have important things to discuss, and already you know something of it."

"Yes," Carlos nodded, "I know that you are now well, and that you will be married, and that you are again driving the trucks. This means that our father has no one to help him work the land."

The teacher looked sharply at Carlos and at Edmundo. Carlos was no longer a child, he could see. Also, he was no fool, and had come to the heart of the matter immediately.

"That is so," answered Edmundo. "Our father has told me to remind you of this. You know he cannot really continue to work the land alone. Martita is young and still in school."

He stopped and played with his food, letting Carlos take his time. He knew Carlos could insist that he was a man, too, doing a man's work already. A man in Lima didn't have to return to his father to work the land in the *altiplano*.

But there was more than this. It had been ingrained over the years in the young men of the *altiplano* that the family was more than a nest that could be left easily. There was the small piece of land to hold them together, and with it was a home.

Carlos had been thinking, but his feelings were strong

and he was almost angry. Would his father want to make a child of him once more? Why didn't Edmundo stay to work the land and bring his new wife to Urubamba? Why couldn't his parents and his grandmother and sister come to Lima? So many came from the mountains, day after day.

He had so much to think over. So many questions. He had learned to love Lima, though his work was monotonous and would lead him nowhere. Still, what could he say now? Could he say goodbye to Lima and return to Urubamba, obediently like a child? Or could he refuse his father and quarrel with his brother? His thoughts crowded one upon the other, and Carlos, silent, eating slowly and thoughtfully, had no answer.

Señor Valdez had been watching the two young men and listening to the conversation. He knew something of what ran through Carlos' mind. He knew that the answers would not be easy for him, whatever he decided. One thing was plain: Carlos did not face a command to be obeyed blindly. The decision was still his to make. So much had the times changed for the people, even for those of the *altiplano*.

"Listen, Edmundo," said Señor Valdez, "Carlos will need to think about what you have said. He can talk with his friends about what he should do, and he can decide. Surely he doesn't have to make up his mind before he eats his dessert!"

Edmundo smiled and leaned back in his chair. He had made his plans and his decisions. He had consulted no one. But then, a man nearly thirty lives this way. Carlos, whom he truly loved, was nearly fourteen. Carlos was still his father's son and Edmundo's young brother. But, he would surely let Carlos make up his own mind, for no one could force him to return to Urubamba if he decided to stay in Lima.

"Don't forget," answered Edmundo, "Señor Valdez, you have important news to give us yourself."

Carlos turned to the teacher and looked expectantly at him. What else could there be?

"How can I forget," said Señor Valdez, "since for this I am in Lima, and it is truly important.

"You remember," he went on, "how we were hoping to have a larger school, a complete primary school of six years?"

"Yes," said Carlos, remembering the old excitement, "and how the people were going to sign a petition for the Ministry of Education in Lima. But there was the opposition of the alcalde, the *hacendado,* and the storekeeper . . ."

"And remember," broke in Edmundo, "how Señor Valdez and Padre Manya tried to convince the gentlemen that education was important to Urubamba? But such stubborn people! Even my friends and I couldn't bring them to understand that another teacher and a larger school were needed."

"Well," continued Señor Valdez, "that is how it was. The people were afraid of the anger of Don Mario and Don Manuel. And Señor Rivera, in his shop, could cause trouble for some of them about their debts."

Carlos felt as if it were only yesterday that he had sat with the teacher and the priest and the others, and listened to their planning and urging of support for the petition. He remembered his excitement at being permitted to listen to their discussions and to run errands for these two important people of his village.

"Then," continued the teacher, "things began to happen. Padre Manya paid a visit to an important person in Cuzco. And I visited a particular friend in the office of the *prefecto,* the governor of the department of Cuzco. After those visits, the three gentlemen were quickly persuaded that they should cooperate with their neighbors.

"It was just a short time afterward that we were greeted by Señor Rivera, who asked pleasantly about the petition.

He wanted to join his friends of Urubamba, and would sign his name to the paper along with the *campesinos*. His thumbprints would not be needed. He had an education and could write!

"And now, our petitions, with names and thumbprints, are complete. The people have all signed, and so have Don Diego and Don Manuel."

"But Señor Valdez," broke in Carlos, "how did they come to change their minds, these important men? Only a short time before, they were angry, and they said your school was fine enough for Urubamba as it is."

"I think they were reminded how right the people were. They learned that education is important and needs always to be improved. They were finally convinced that people who can read and write work better with more tools and with better ones. They might even be better customers in a store."

He looked at Edmundo, who nodded his head solemnly in agreement. Then Señor Valdez went on.

"They even learned that other towns with better schools grew prosperous and that people moved away from little towns with poor schools."

"That is so," agreed Carlos, still stunned by the news that the important men of the town had joined their cause.

"And now, Señor Valdez, what happens now?" he asked.

"That is why I've come to Lima," answered the teacher. "I have the petitions, and together with Don Francisco, our *diputado* in the congress, I will take them to the Ministry of Education. Would you like to see them?"

They went to Señor Valdez' room again and there he spread out for them all the pages and pages of petitions. They were official-looking documents, with seals and places marked off for the names of each signer. Carlos remembered how bare some of these sheets had looked. And now they were neatly ruled off, with the many thumbprints and signatures.

"We're very proud of these papers," said Señor Valdez, "and you should be also. After all, without your help, nothing could have been done."

Carlos felt pleased with the praise of the teacher. He still remembered the day of his *promoción,* when after only four years of school, he and his friends had finished their education in Urubamba. Now, maybe there would be a larger school and another teacher. What excitement for the children of the town!

They talked about the idea of building more classrooms.

"Already," said the teacher, "the parents are working on the building."

Then he added, smiling, "If they were not cautioned, they would build five more rooms instead of only the two that we need. One is for the last two grades of school, and the other is for the teacher to live in. But you know how our people are when they are enthusiastic about a project. They work with all their hearts."

Then, looking at Edmundo and Carlos, Señor Valdez realized it was quite late. He thought they would want more time to talk and make their own plans.

"Carlos," he said, "however you decide about yourself, I know you will think seriously first. You should know that if you return to Urubamba, you will not just work the land with your father. There will be work for you with me at the school. Did you think your education was ended just because you came to Lima? I will need you also, and so will Padre Manya. You would have a welcome from us that would never wear out."

Suddenly Carlos felt as if his eyes had just opened. He had imagined himself a worker on the land, a *campesino,* a follower of the sheep. These few words of Señor Valdez had brought a new picture to his mnid. Just a short time spent with his brother and his teacher had brought him problems he had not expected. Now he would have to think deeply and try to do the right thing.

He and Edmundo got up to leave. They agreed to meet again for dinner tomorrow evening. Señor Valdez would tell them of his visit to the ministry and then he would plan to return to Urubamba.

As they drove back to the Fernandez house, to Carlos' room, he and Edmundo spoke only briefly. Edmundo told him he would be driving a truck to Arequipa in the next few days. He hoped they might visit Rosita again before he left. Carlos felt quiet and restrained, almost resentful toward his brother, but he realized deep in his heart that this was not just. His brother was no boy, and he was entitled to make his own way in life. Besides, the short time they had spent with Señor Valdez had given him a strange renewed feeling of happiness about his village.

When they reached the house, Carlos asked his brother to come in and see his room. This would show him how well he could live in Lima, even if he was just a sweeper, a wrapper, an errand boy.

They went quietly into the house, and as they sat and talked in his room, they were interrupted by a knock at the door. It was Julia. She greeted Carlos and shyly glanced at his visitor.

"Carlito," she said, "wouldn't you want to join Hipólito and me in the kitchen? We have coffee for you and your guest."

Moved by her kindness, Carlos presented his brother, and they went to sit with her and Hipólito.

"My husband and I have been happy that your young brother is with us, Don Edmundo," she said.

"No, señora," answered the driver, "I am not Don, only Edmundo, who might even be your son."

"We have no son," answered Hipólito, "but Carlos is a good boy and a hard worker. He comes from a good family."

"*Ay*, we are *campesinos*," said Edmundo. "My father works his bit of land in Urubamba, near Cuzco."

He stopped just then and didn't want to look at Carlos. But Carlos was with people who knew him and whom he loved and respected.

"My brother has brought me news," he said. "Our father wishes me to return to Urubamba and work with him on the land. My brother is an important *piloto*. He drives great trucks on the highways, and my father now needs my help."

He spoke proudly of his brother, as he always had, and Edmundo felt this now and was glad to know what Carlos really thought.

"So," said Julia, "you must leave us and the Señora, and return to your family."

"No," said Carlos, almost violently, "it is not a matter of 'must'! I can do as I wish. I work and earn my way in life. Why do you say 'must'?"

"Julia does not say you must, Carlito," said Hipólito. "Of course it is your decision."

But Carlos felt that Julia had spoken to him as his mother would have. And that, again, Hipólito's words might have been his father's. His feelings seemed to be fighting with his desires. Perhaps, after all, the "must" was what he wanted for himself.

While the others talked about Edmundo's work, about life in the country and in the city, Carlos listened vaguely, and the feeling of doubt was all he knew.

Soon Edmundo said, "I must go now. It is quite late and I am staying in the home of some friends who will be waiting for me."

Then, turning to his brother, he said warmly, "Carlito,

it has been quite a day for you. I hope you will sleep well. I will come to the *farmacia* again in the afternoon. I'm sure Señora Fernandez will give you a few more hours of time off for me."

Carlos couldn't help smiling. He shook his brother's hand firmly and looked into his eyes.

"*Hasta mañana*, 'Mundo," he said.

12

THAT NIGHT CARLOS LAY IN HIS BED, UNABLE TO SLEEP. He saw in his mind the many happy times he and Ricardo had known in Lima. He remembered the sights and the sounds and the smells they had enjoyed, and he felt that this was his home forever.

Then he remembered his days at the *Farmacia* Fernandez, where his work was simple and required very little of him, except his time and his strength. Could he learn to manage the store? There was Señorita Ysabel who had been to high school. There were the Señor and Señora Fernandez, too. The store had plenty of managers.

He couldn't work and go to school, not in Lima, not unless he had another job. Then he remembered all the men who spent their time in the *parque* and in the plazas waiting for news of a job, and he knew he couldn't join them. He had no trade, no skills, except those of a *campesino* or of a drugstore errand boy.

As he tossed in his bed, he thought of the happy times he had spent with Pablo's family, with the boys and with Doña Maria. Could he go to school in Lima and live with them in the *barriada,* eating rice he had not earned, adding to the crowd who already huddled in the ramshackle hut with a dirt floor and no water?

As he went over all his experiences since leaving Urubamba, he decided that without more education, he could do nothing more. He could be an errand boy as long as they wanted to keep him. Then, if he should somehow displease the Señora, he could join the *pájaros* again, or the crowds of boys who shined shoes and sold lottery tickets in the plaza.

With luck he might work as a *chulillo*, and then become a *piloto*. Edmundo had done it. But even Edmundo wanted to leave the highways and settle down. And Carlos remembered how Don Vicente had encouraged him to study and to do better for himself.

"No, *hombre*," the driver had said, "this is for men who have little learning, who can drive until the mud stops the truck, and who can clean up after the people and their chickens."

Carlos turned from side to side, finding no rest.

He thought of his parents and his grandmother. His father would be going to the fields each day, to plant, to pull weeds, to watch the sky for rain, and to separate the stones from the soil.

He remembered Martita, who was still in school, but who would marry in a few years as did most of the girls of the *altiplano*. He could see her cheery face, her fat cheeks, and her smiling eyes.

Carlos could almost hear the music of his *quena*, as he watched the sheep grazing in their pasture. Was he to be a shepherd boy and a *campesino* after all, and nothing more?

With Edmundo gone, his father needed him, and Carlos felt this thought stronger than all the others. His father could not go on working the land alone, and there was no money to pay a man to work with him as if he were one of the sons. His father needed him.

Then, with a leaping heart, he remembered what the teacher had said. "I will need you also, and so will Padre Manya."

With a new school, there would be many things to do. Carlos, too, would be at the school. He would finish his years of *primaria* and then, maybe there might even be a *colegio,* or high school, in Urubamba. Who knows what the people could do? Look what a petition with thumbprints could produce!

Now, in his narrow bed, in the dark little room, Carlos' thoughts raced, and now he did not miss his sleep. He could see himself with his family, working with his father, joking and laughing with his sister and his friends. He could tell stories to the boys about Lima and about the *Cóndor,* how they drove the highways furiously, and how they waited for the people to dig the road free of the landslide. He could tell about the streets and buildings, the airport and the docks of the harbor. He would be proud of his work in Lima and of his many adventures. What other boys could tell as much, truthfully?

Tomorrow he would tell Edmundo and Señor Valdez of his decision to return to Urubamba. The thought suddenly gave him a feeling of ease and comfort. He felt as if he had no troubles and no concerns to worry him. With a sigh, he turned over on his side and, finally, he slept.

The next days passed quickly and with excitement for Carlos. He told Edmundo and Señor Valdez what he would do: he was returning to his family. He told Señora Fernandez that she would have to find another errand boy and he would leave in a few days. Of course, she was angry. She would have to teach a new boy all that Carlos had learned to do so well. *Ay,* these *campesinos,* she thought. But she agreed to let him stay in his room until he left Lima, if it would be only for a few days. Julia and Hipólito had asked her very respectfully for this special favor to them.

Carlos visited Ricardo and Sarita for the last time. Ricardo embraced him as they said goodbye. "Carlito, why should you leave Lima? Look at us, we are happy here, and we are saving our money to go into business someday. Must you go back to little Urubamba again?"

Carlos felt a pang, but he had decided. Ricardo's life was not his. And Ricardo had brothers who were in Urubamba to help their parents with their work. No, it wasn't the same.

When Carlos went to the *barriada* to visit the family of Doña Maria and to say farewell to Pablo, he brought some packages of food and materials for clothing which Doña Maria would sew. He looked for their shack, and when he found it, there was another family living in it.

Carlos asked the woman who sat by the doorway about Doña Maria, and she looked at him suspiciously.

"What do you want with them?" she asked. "You can see they are not here!"

"Please, señora, they are old friends. I have some things for them. Can't you tell me where they are?"

The woman continued to sit, and she gazed about her defiantly.

"I don't know. One of the boys was caught by the police, and then the family moved away. This is our house and I have nothing more to tell you."

Carlos left sadly, wondering what could have happened to his friends who had been so kind to him. When a boy was caught by the police, he was often beaten and sent away to work. He shuddered to think of Pablo without his family, and especially without his mother.

He wandered over to the Plaza San Martín and to the Plaza Bolívar. Surely, here among the shoeshine boys and the lottery-ticket sellers, he could find some news. But none of the boys he asked would tell him anything. Most of them knew no Pablo of that *barriada*. One boy thought they might have moved up to another *barriada, el Montón*, but he wasn't sure and couldn't say where Carlos would find Doña Maria.

Wearily, Carlos returned home and gave the packages back to Julia, telling her what had happened.

"Carlito," she said, "they were good to you. Let us hope that others will be good to them. It is sad for so many people like them."

She could say no more, and it did not help Carlos' sorrowful mood.

The rest of the days that remained he spent with Edmundo, with Rosa, and with Señor Valdez. The teacher told them with triumph in his voice how he had gone with the *diputado* to the ministry, directly to the office of the director of all primary schools in Peru. They had been received with courtesy, and their petition had been accepted. Later he had been called to a meeting at the director's office, and he had met not only the director, but another official, a North American.

"Señor Valdez," said the director, "this is Señor Wilson, who is with the *Cuerpo de Paz*, the Peace Corps, of the United States. We have something to discuss with you."

The North American spoke almost perfect Spanish, and then came the surprise. Señor Valdez was told that the Ministry of Education had invited young North Americans of the *Cuerpo de Paz* to go to the *altiplano* and help as teachers. They would live in the villages, work among the people, and be teachers in the schools.

"After all, *maestro*," said the director, "you know how few teachers we have who can go to the villages. Would you and the people of Urubamba accept this collaboration from our friends?"

"Señor Director," answered Señor Valdez in a respectful tone, and looking also at Señor Wilson, "we don't know these people, and we were hoping for a Peruvian to teach our children."

"Of course," replied the director, "but the supply of trained teachers is sadly small. You know this also. The people of the *Cuerpo de Paz* speak excellent Spanish. Some of them have been teachers in their own country. And they are willing to work with you in the school. I do not know how we can answer the petition of Urubamba now in any other way."

Señor Wilson added at this point, "Our people are volunteers. They are well trained and their Spanish is good. They are not tourists. We have sent such volunteers to teach in schools all over the world. You may remember one of my colleagues, Dr. Taylor, who visited Urubamba recently. He believes the volunteers can be of help. I hope you will let them show you...."

Señor Valdez smiled and replied, "If we need a teacher and one volunteers to come to us, well then, let us see how well he can work. Our people and their children need teachers. Maybe there are many things they can learn from the North Americans that even a Peruvian cannot teach."

Carlos and Edmundo listened to this story and were pleased that the petition of Urubamba would be accepted and that a new teacher would be sent. But Carlos wasn't very sure about these *gringos*. He wondered how they would like living in a small village, among *campesinos*. Well, if Señor Valdez was hopeful, he would be also. If they had volunteered to teach, maybe they would be willing to learn.

At last, the day came for his departure. Early in the morning, Julia and Hipólito awakened Carlos. A huge breakfast was ready for him, along with a small box of food of all kinds for the journey. They could not leave the house, and Julia wept when she embraced Carlos for the last time. Hipólito, almost as silent as ever, shook his hand and put his arms around the boy, letting him feel his strong emotions. Carlos promised he would write, and they would be seeing Edmundo from time to time.

At the Parque Universitario, the first thing they saw was the *Cóndor Dorado* and the smiling Don Vicente.

"Good morning, my fine passenger!" he exclaimed and shook hands with Carlos.

He greeted Edmundo and Rosa also, saying that he hoped the weather and the roads would be favorable.

"*Ay*, Carlos," he said, "do you remember how we waited to pass the roadblock? You were a fresh young *chulillo* then!"

Carlos smiled and handed his packages to Juanito, the boy who helped Don Vicente now on the *Cóndor*. He felt strange about riding inside the great bus instead of climbing up above to lie with the baggage. He promised himself that at least for a few hours on the trip, he would join Juanito. That is, if Don Vicente would give his permission.

While they waited for Señor Valdez, Rosa took Carlos aside and spoke with him seriously.

"I know you are doing what is right, Carlito," she said, "and your brother is proud of you for it."

"I will be glad to help my *taita* in the fields again," Carlos replied, "but I know I will miss Lima."

"Edmundo and I have decided also that after we are married, you could come to Lima and spend some holidays with us, Carlito."

Carlos' eyes sparkled at the idea.

"Then, later on," she added, "if God is willing, there might even be a way for you to come to Lima and live with us while you go to school."

Carlos could say nothing. He knew that if Edmundo's plans succeeded, there might be enough money to pay a man who would work on the land. If the times were good, if one's plans went well. If, if . . .

He looked at his future sister, and her unselfish thoughts made her dear to him. They would see what the future brought.

Just then Señor Valdez arrived in a taxi with two men and several large boxes. Señor Valdez ordered Juanito to be

very careful with the boxes, and Don Vicente scowled at him for giving orders to his *chulillo*.

Then the teacher presented the two strangers. They were the Peace Corps volunteers, all ready and prepared to travel to the *altiplano* with them. They were Señor Klein and Señor Lewis, teachers for Urubamba, and they were bringing books and pencils and paper, and many other things needed in a school.

What an excitement there will be when we arrive, thought Carlos. We are really bringing the school to Urubamba with us!

At last it was time to leave. Carlos looked at his brother. Edmundo was warm and serious, knowing Rosa had already spoken to Carlos of their plans. They embraced once more. Then, inside the bus, all the passengers, for Ica, for Nazca, for Cuzco, for Urubamba, were seated. The *chulillo* rapped on the window from his ladder in the back. Don Vicente sounded his horn loudly and with great power, and the *Cóndor* moved into the traffic on the streets of Lima.

Carlos closed his eyes and leaned back in his seat. The sounds and smells of Lima were on all sides. He didn't know when he would ever return, but as he listened, he felt the surge of the bus. Already he could feel the power of the *Cóndor Dorado* as it made its way upward with him, into the mountains, toward his future.

Glossary

abuelita	grandmother [affectionate]
abuelito	grandfather [affectionate]
adiós	goodbye
ají	pepper [very hot!]
alcalde	mayor
altiplano	highlands
alumnos	students
ex-alumnos	graduates
anticucho	meat or fish cooked and eaten on a skewer
ari	yes [Quechua, the ancient Inca language]
ay	an exclamation [like "ow!"]
barriada	neighborhood, district
barrio	neighborhood, district
bien	well, good
buenos días	good day, good morning
butifarra	sandwich
caldo	soup
campesino	farmer, peasant
caray	exclamation [like "gosh!"]
carretera	highway
centavos	cents
chicha	strong beer made of corn
chico	young fellow, "my lad"
cholo	Indian [a "country" type of person]
chulillo	helper [a mischievous "monkey"]
chullo	knitted cap [Quechua]

churi	my son [Quechua]
churrasco	broiled meat, steak
colectivo	a taxi that runs on a route like a bus
colegio	high school in Peru
compañero	friend, chum
con	with
cóndor dorado	golden condor
con permiso	excuse me [very polite]
Cuerpo de Paz	Peace Corps
Dios y Patria	God and Country
diputado	deputy, congressman
director	director, principal of a school
Don	Mr. [very respectful]
Doña	Mrs. [very respectful]
familia	family, household
farmacia	pharmacy, drugstore
fútbol	soccer [not U.S.-style football!]
gracias	thanks
grado	level [in school]
Gran Lima	Great Lima [the capital of Peru]
gringo	foreigner [not friendly, usually said of a North American from the U.S.A.]
guardia civil	police
hacendado	landowner [of a hacienda]
hacienda	farm, plantation
hasta mañana	goodbye [until tomorrow]
hola	hello, hi!
hombre	man
jirón, jirónes	street, streets [in Peru, for the oldest streets in the city]
kilo	weight, short for kilogram [metric weight: about 2.2 pounds]

Lima	the capital city of Peru
Limeño	a citizen of Lima
maestro	teacher, boss, master
mañana	morning, tomorrow
manta	shawl
marinera	a folk dance
mayordomo	the chief servant in a house
mercado	market
mercadito	little market
montaña	mountain [in Peru, can also be jungle area]
muchas	much, many
padre	father
pájaro	bird
pájaros fruteros	tricky boys who steal in the markets
Parque Universitario	University Park
permiso	permission
piloto	driver
Plaza de Armas	the main square of a town or city
pobrecito	poor little one!
poncho	a blanketlike cloak with a slit in the middle for the head
prefecto	prefect, a high official
primaria	first year in school
primer	first
promoción	graduation
quena	flute [Quechua], usually of reeds
Qué tal?	How are you?
reata	rope, lasso
segundo	second
señor	sir, mister
señora	Mrs. madame

señores	gentlemen
señorita	miss, young lady
señorito	young gentleman [sometimes not friendly]
sol	sun; Peruvian money
soles	money
taita	father [Quechua]
tierra	land
toreros	bullfighters
Vaya con Dios!	Go with God!

AUTHORS GUILD BACKINPRINT.COM EDITIONS are fiction and nonfiction works that were originally brought to the reading public by established United States publishers but have fallen out of print. The economics of traditional publishing methods force tens of thousands of works out of print each year, eventually claiming many, if not most, award-winning and one-time best-selling titles. With improvements in print-on-demand technology, authors and their estates, in cooperation with the Authors Guild, are making some of these works available again to readers in quality paperback editions. Authors Guild Backinprint.com Editions may be found at nearly all online bookstores and are also available from traditional booksellers. For further information or to purchase any Backinprint.com title please visit www.backinprint.com.

Except as noted on their copyright pages, Authors Guild Backinprint.com Editions are presented in their original form. Some authors have chosen to revise or update their works with new information. The Authors Guild is not the editor or publisher of these works and is not responsible for any of the content of these editions.

THE AUTHORS GUILD is the nation's largest society of published book authors. Since 1912 it has been the leading writers' advocate for fair compensation, effective copyright protection, and free expression. Further information is available at www.authorsguild.org.

Please direct inquiries about the Authors Guild and Backinprint.com Editions to the Authors Guild offices in New York City, or e-mail staff@backinprint.com.

Printed in the United States
132065LV00001B/192/A